THE FACTORY GIRL'S SONG

Victorian Romance

FAYE GODWIN

Tica House
Publishing

Sweet Romance that Delights and Enchants!

PERSONAL WORD FROM THE AUTHOR

Dearest Readers,

I'm so delighted that you have chosen one of my books to read. I am proud to be a part of the team of writers at Tica House Publishing. Our goal is to inspire, entertain, and give you many hours of reading pleasure. Your kind words and loving readership are deeply appreciated.

I would like to personally invite you to sign up for updates and to become part of our **Exclusive Reader Club**—it's completely Free to Join! I'd love to welcome you!

Much love,

Faye Godwin

VISIT HERE to Join our Reader's Club and to Receive Tica House Updates:

http://ticahousepublishing.subscribemenow.com

PART I

CHAPTER 1

Olive knew that Father was getting worse.

She watched him as he walked across their tiny tenement, keeping her head ducked, her dirty and stringy dark hair falling over her eyes as she tried to scrub the floor. She didn't want him to know that she knew how sick he was – it would only make him and Mother worry even more.

Still, she knew by the way he moved that his entire body was aching. He didn't so much walk as drag himself, his thin frame staggering across the grubby floor. Everything about him seemed to rattle: his thin shoulders in their sockets, his bruised fingers against each other, his breath as it struggled in and out of a chest clogged with sickness. When he sat down, slowly, on the upturned bucket that was all they had for a chair, his frame seemed to shrink. He seemed so... defeated. Like life had given him one beating too many.

Father looked up. Olive hurriedly turned back to her work, moving the dry brush across the floor with all of her might. It was a tattered thing, its last few bristles scraping pathetically on the wooden floor, not so much removing the grime as simply raking a few scratches in it. Olive wondered how many families had stayed here in this tiny tenement, how much death and disease this little room had seen. How much of it was here on the floor, where she knelt in her ragged dress, her thin arms forcing the brush down harder and harder.

She wished she could scrub it away – all of it - the illness that had changed her strong and lively father into this skeleton of a man. The worry that had worn lines around her mother's eyes, aging her ten years in a matter of months. The way that hunger had stolen the plump cheeks of her little brother Jimmy, himself reduced to a scrawny shadow of the bouncing five-year-old he had been before the illness came for Father.

Olive knew she wasn't supposed to notice these things. She was only eight years old, after all. But she did, and the sight of them weighed on her soul.

"Olive." Her father's voice was gentle. "Why don't you stop there? I don't think..." He paused. "I don't think there's much more you can do right now."

Olive took a deep breath and laid down the brush.

"Hello, Father," she said. It took all of her courage to smile. Sometimes the weight of their poverty felt like it was crushing her, small as she was, but she couldn't let Father see her suffer. She went over to him and laid a small hand on his bony knee. "How are you doing today?"

"Better, love." Father always gave the same answer, even as Olive watched him wasting away. "Much better."

He took her into his skinny arms and drew her into a lap that was little more than two leg bones wrapped in skin. It was still the safest place that Olive could think of. She tucked her head under his chin and felt his arms surround her.

"What is the matter, Olive?" Father asked gently. His chest was nothing but a basket frame of bone where it moved against her as he breathed. "You used to run to greet me at the door when I come home from work."

Olive turned her face into his chest. She couldn't tell him the truth – that every time he came home, his pale face terrified her. "I'm sorry, Father. I-I just want to clean our room."

Father sighed. Olive watched as he looked around the tiny place that they had been calling home for several months, ever since he lost his job gardening at the rich man's house. The old man had provided them with comfortable servants' quarters, but when he'd died and his arrogant son had taken over, they had been unceremoniously thrown out.

Now, they lived in this tenement, a creaking place on the top floor of a moth-eaten building. There was one straw mattress where Father slept with Jimmy. Olive and Mother had a couple of blankets and lay beside it; Olive had always seen Mother's fingers entangled with Father's skeletal hand on the edge of the mattress. The entire place was covered in a layer of nameless dirt. Some of it had to be soot from one of the nearby factories. Olive didn't dare to imagine what the rest of it was, or why it smelt the way it did.

"Oh, Olive." Father sighed, kissing the top of her head. "You do your best. You're a good girl." He cuddled her a little closer. "Where's your mother?"

"She went to take back the mending," Olive told him.

"Of course. When..." Father had to pause as a fit of coughing seized him, shaking his entire frame so that Olive almost fell off his lap. "When did she leave?"

"Almost two hours ago. She'll be back soon."

As Olive spoke, there was a cacophony of creaking and screeching as the wooden stairs struggled under the weight of someone coming up to the top floor. She heard her mother's warm voice and Jimmy's piping tone accompanying her. The front door opened, and her tousle-haired little brother stood framed in the doorway, his pinched cheeks pale in the watery wisps of sunlight that managed to wander in through the single window. When he saw Father, his little face lit up in unadulterated joy.

"Father!" He ran across the room in two long bounds and tumbled into Father's lap beside Olive.

Father laughed. "Come here, my little wild thing." He kissed Jimmy's head, studying him. There was sorrow in his eyes.

"John?" Mother's voice was frightened. Olive looked up at her, feeling her heartbeat quicken with fright. Mother's brown eyes were wide, the color drained from her face. She held an armful of clothes for mending. "What are you doing here?"

"Molly." Father rose, gently pushing the two children to the floor. Both solemn with fear, they clung to each other as Father crossed the floor with painful slowness. He reached out, laying a hand on each of Mother's shoulders. "I'm so sorry."

Mother's face crumpled like a crushed flower. The clothes fell to the floor with a dull thud as she raised her hands to her mouth. "What happened?" Her voice was a thin croak of horror.

"I tried, Molly. I promise you." Father's voice broke. "I-I couldn't stop..." He glanced over at the children. "The men on the docks turned a blind eye to the coughing," he said, his voice lower. "But today one of the supervisors spotted me coughing up..." He glanced at Jimmy again, and only mouthed the next word, but Olive saw it clearly. *Blood.* "They said I was too sick to be any good."

"No. No." Mother was shaking her head, tears pouring down her cheeks. "It can't be. How are we going to survive?"

"I'm so sorry, Molly." Father's voice was shattered, rough. "I will find other work. Everyone on the docks will know by now, but maybe one of the factories..."

Mother was already shaking her head. "It's no good. You're too sick." Her tone was matter-of-fact. She dashed her tears away, squaring her shoulders as she swallowed her sobs. "We'll manage. We'll find a way somehow."

She bent down, gathering the mending back into her arms, and shot Olive and Jimmy a smile that Olive knew was supposed to console them. It didn't.

"I have the mending," she said cheerfully.

Father nodded, his smile strained. "Your cousin was very good to get you work from the estate where she works."

"She was," said Mother. "Come on, Olive." She hoisted the pile higher in her arms and fixed Olive with a look that held a hardness that Olive hadn't seen there before. It was made of steel, and it scared her. "I'm getting paid by the piece, so you're going to learn how to mend. We're going to hold this family together." Her voice quivered. "We're going to hold it all together."

CHAPTER 2

The wind howled through the broken windowpane, bringing with it little eddies of snow that made the freezing tenement even colder. Olive's fingers were blue and numb as she crouched next to their mattress, a chipped bowl in one hand, a wooden spoon in the other. The watery broth in the bowl had been little more than lukewarm to begin with – coal was a precious commodity that they used in tiny pieces when they needed it. Now, with the temperature in the tenement plunging, it was almost ice cold. Olive wondered if it would freeze over. She pushed the idea out of her mind and held out the spoon to Father, trying not to let her shivers cause any of the broth to drip onto his ragged shirt.

"One more, Father," she whispered, her thin voice pleading. "Just one more."

Father's face had once been strong and tanned, creased by smile lines. Now it looked more and more like a naked skull with every passing day. Feverish eyes burned deep in their sockets as he stared up at Olive, trying to smile. Every breath seemed to take more effort than he had. He shook his head, and even that small movement seemed to tire him, draining the little color that had been left in his face.

"Please, Father." Olive trembled, holding the spoon a little nearer to his lips. "For me."

Weakly, her father opened his mouth. Olive struggled to spoon the broth inside, hoping that some of it was going down. He coughed, the sound wet and broken, and wiped his hand across his mouth. A smear of blood was left on the back of his hand.

"Thank you," he murmured as Olive set down the bowl. "You're a good girl." His eyes searched hers. "I'm sorry."

"Hush." Olive pulled the thin blanket closer over her father's shoulders. "Sleep now. You'll feel better."

Father closed his eyes, and Olive sat down next to the mattress, exhausted. She stared dully at the broken pane, the frost collecting around its edges. They'd already plugged the worst of the holes in the walls with crumpled bits of discarded newspaper, but the broken windowpane was just too big. She was so hungry. As soon as Father's breathing settled into the rhythm of sleep, she grabbed the bowl and tipped it up directly into her mouth. The broth was so cold that it slid down her throat like swallowed ice.

Jimmy lay on his belly in the middle of the floor, playing with three matchsticks. Olive's heart ached as she watched him moving the matchsticks across the floor, pretending they were horses and soldiers. Once, back in those warm servants' quarters, Jimmy had possessed wooden horses and balls to play with. All that had long since been pawned for rent or sold for food.

Noticing Olive's gaze on him, Jimmy sat up. "There's nothing to do," he announced.

Olive tried not to stare too hard at him. It seemed that he was getting thinner and paler every day. At least he still had the vigor of any five-year-old boy cooped up in a tiny room all of the time – although sometimes she wished he didn't.

"Play with your matches, Jimmy," she said, mustering her patience.

"Isn't there anything else we can do?" Jimmy came over and sat down beside her. She saw worry in his brown eyes, so similar to their mother's. "I'm tired of being stuck in here."

"I know. Me, too." Olive found a smile for him. "Let's a sing a song."

Jimmy clapped his hands. "Yes, yes! What will we sing?"

Olive began to make up a song on the spot, clapping her hands in rhythm to the tune. It was a song about the birds and flowers that she remembered so clearly from their previous home. She and Jimmy had played for hours in the beautiful garden that her father kept, listening to him as he talked about all the different plants. He knew everything there was to know about every living thing that could be found in a garden, from the tiniest seed to the furry rabbits that occasionally hopped across the lawn.

Now all of that was gone, but Olive squeezed her eyes tight shut, trying to summon her memories of that better, happier, more beautiful time, trying to bring one golden thread of joy and contentment into the cold and hunger of their dirty little tenement.

Jimmy's high-pitched voice joined her, and Olive tried to pretend that they were back there in the garden in the time before their master had died. She reached out as she sang and took hold of Jimmy's hand. Once it had been soft and chubby to the touch; now it was chapped from the cold, the bones sliding under his thin skin. Olive squeezed it and tried to dream herself away into a time of warmth and abundance, a time when Jimmy had been rosy-cheeked, her father strong, her mother cheerful.

The sound of the tenement door opening brought their song to a stop. Jimmy jumped up, snatching his hand out of Olive's.

"Mother!" he cried, and rushed across the room. Before he could reach her, he was gripped by a fit of coughing that doubled him over. The coughs were wet and harsh, a raw, painful sound.

Mother's brow creased in concern. She crossed the distance between the doorway and Jimmy in two long strides, scooping him up into her arms. Her lips were blue with cold as she kissed his forehead. "Jimmy, love, what's the matter?" She pressed her hand against his forehead. "Are you all right?"

Jimmy wiped his mouth. "I'm hungry."

"I know, my love." Mother sighed, gently setting Jimmy back onto the floor.

"Did you bring us something to eat?" asked Olive. She shot a glance over at her father, who was still asleep, his doze uninterrupted by the noise of Mother's arrival. "We just finished the broth."

"I did." Mother smiled and took a drawstring bag down from where it had been slung over her shoulder. It was a mismatched thing, cobbled together from extra bits of material she used for the mending. "Here." She pulled the bag open and lifted out a loaf of bread. It looked hard and dry, but Jimmy rushed forward, his little hands snatching at it, and Mother pushed him away.

"Wait, Jimmy," she said firmly. "We all have to eat. I do have a special treat for you today, though."

"What is it, Mother?" asked Olive, whose mouth was watering at the sight of the bread.

Mother reached into the bag again and drew out something that Olive hadn't tasted in months: an apple. It was a red and rosy thing, suddenly bright and vibrant in their colorless tenement. Jimmy's mouth formed an O of excitement. He stretched up his arms toward it.

"Oooh, an apple," he whispered.

Olive stared at the fruit, her heart suddenly hammering. She thought back to a few weeks ago, when she and Mother had been walking through the streets together to take back the finished mending. There had been a huge crowd assembled on one of the street corners.

"Come on, Mother," Olive had said, tugging her mother's hand in the direction of the crowd. "Let's go and see what's happening there. Maybe there's a musician or a singer." Olive adored music, and there was little to be had in their dinghy corner of Old Nichol.

Mother looked up, and a look of dread crossed her face. She shuddered, pulling Olive back. "No, no, my dear. We're in too much of a hurry. Come."

"Why not?" Olive stopped. "Please. Can't we just go and see?"

Mother's expression softened. She bent down, putting a hand on Olive's shoulder. "There's no musician there, Olive. There's a hanging."

Olive didn't know what a hanging was, but the way her mother said the word made her scared. "What's that?"

"It's…" Mother paused. "It's a very, very bad punishment."

Olive turned her head, trying to see past the crowd. All she could see was a long wooden scaffold with a rope hanging fairly loosely from it. "Why are they punishing someone there?"

"I don't know." Mother straightened, grabbing Olive's hand. "Probably a thief."

They hurried off back into the dirty streets, but Olive glanced back once. And it was just in time to see the rope springing tight with the body dangling below, and to hear the terrible, gurgling, choking sound reach her over the heads of the silent crowd.

Now, looking at the apple in Mother's hand, Olive knew that the sound she'd heard had been somebody dying. She also knew that there was no way that Mother's cousin's mistress had paid her so much for the mending that she could have bought an apple on the way home. She looked into Mother's eyes, picturing her own mother standing on that scaffold with the rope around her neck. What would she and Jimmy do then?

"Where did you get it, Mother?" she whispered.

"At the market," said Mother briskly. "Now come. Let's cut it up into four and share it."

"Father won't want any," Jimmy piped up. "He didn't even finish the broth that Olive was giving him." He turned his large, liquid eyes on Mother. "Why won't he eat, Mother? Is he getting sicker?"

Olive read the answer in Mother's frightened eyes. "Don't worry your head about it, Jimmy," she ordered, cutting the apple. "Here. Take some bread, too."

Jimmy snatched the piece of apple from Mother's hand and sat down in a corner, devouring it in a few starving bites. Olive hesitantly took her piece and bit off the end. It was wonderfully sweet.

"Mother?" she said, quietly, hoping Jimmy somehow wouldn't hear. "Father is getting worse, isn't he?"

The lines on Mother's face seemed to deepen as she looked at Olive. "Yes," she said softly. "I'm afraid he is."

"Then why don't we get the doctor?"

"Oh, Olive." Mother ran a hand over her face, pushing her mousy hair out of her eyes. "You know we can't afford that."

"But he's not getting better," Olive insisted. "Winter's coming, and it's only getting colder and dirtier in here. What if..." She swallowed. "What if he..."

"Hush, Olive," Mother ordered, her face hardening as she straightened up. "Eat your supper. I don't want to hear another word out of you."

Mother's tone was angry. But the expression in her face and eyes clearly showed fear.

Olive ducked her head, clutching her slice of apple and fistful of bread close to her chest. She made her way over to the mattress and sat cuddled up against it, pressing her cheek against her father's limp arm. Her touch woke him. His eyes opened, and he gazed at her for a few moments, his expression foggy and feverish.

"Are you all right, Father?" Olive whispered.

His bony hand caressed her hair, his touch weak and trembling. "Oh, Olive," he whispered. "You're a good girl. You're..." His eyes started to close, his words slurring as he began to fall back asleep. "You're such a good little girl."

CHAPTER 3

"Here we go round the mulberry bush, the mulberry bush, the mulberry bush," Olive sang. "Here we go round the mulberry bush, on a cold and frosty morning." She skipped in time to the little rhyme, trying to keep warm, the lyrics of the song coming out on puffs of steam. "This is the way we wash our face, wash our face, wash our face..."

Her voice was a thin and trembling wisp of purity and beauty on this terrible street as she clutched Jimmy's hand, tugging him after her, singing louder so that she couldn't hear him coughing. "Comb our hair, comb our hair. This is the way we comb our hair on a cold and frosty morning."

She'd seldom seen a morning colder and frostier than this one. A thin layer of frost sparkled on the road surface, dusting the single pile of horse manure that lay in the middle of the road.

It was about the cleanest thing on the filthy road surface. Every breath Olive took sucked in more of the stench that arose from the debris lining every gutter, scattered across the pavement: rags and old bones, puddles of nameless gunk that had an oily shimmer in the dim morning light, maggoty carcasses of dead rats.

Olive's eyes found the shrunken and faded corpse of a cat, little more than a heap of hair on the pavement. The ragged men and women walking the street just stepped over its broken body as if it was nothing more than the rest of the anonymous filth piled up on the streets. Her stomach turned, and she gagged a little, swallowing down her disgust to sing the next verse. "This is the way we brush our teeth," she sang out as bravely as she could. "Brush our teeth, brush our teeth."

No one on these grubby streets paid her voice any attention. Olive tried not to be scared. She tightened her grip on Jimmy's hand, and he looked up at her, his eyes wide. "Olive, it's not working. Nobody is giving us any money."

"It's not going to work here," said Olive patiently. "Nobody has money to give us."

"Then why did you say you were going to sing for money?"

"Because it'll work once we get to the square," said Olive. "There's rich people there. They'll like my songs, and they'll feel sorry for us and give us money. You'll see."

Jimmy seemed to believe her words more easily than she did. He nodded, his light brown hair bouncing a little. "Then why are you singing now?"

"For fun," said Olive as bravely as she could.

The truth was that she felt that if she didn't sing, she would run – run all the way back to their tenement and its filth and noise, anything rather than these cold streets and the unknown, searching eyes of the people who passed them. But she had to be brave for Father. She pictured him lying on that mattress, nothing more than a sack of bones wrapped in pale skin, the labored rattle of every breath echoing with a desperate certainty around the tiny room. Olive knew that he was dying. But maybe, just maybe, if she could sing well enough today, she would make enough money for a doctor. She clutched Jimmy's hand, wondering where Mother was. She had a plan to save Father, but Mother was a different story.

At last, as they headed up Boundary Street, Olive started to hear the clip-clop of horse-drawn vehicles up ahead. Here in Old Nichol, horse hooves squelched in dirt; the sound of horseshoes on clean cobblestones meant that they were getting closer to the square where Olive planned to sing. Around them, the towering and gloomy tenements began to give way to more cheerful shops.

At last, rounding a corner, they reached the square. The openness of it always lifted Olive's spirits; finally being able to see the sun and the sky reminded her of her beloved garden back in a happy past that was so distant now it felt like it had happened to somebody else. She paused on the street corner, taking in a long breath. She could smell fresh bread from a nearby bakery and wood smoke from the hearth of some privileged family. There were no scents of decay here, except for those that still clung to Olive's ragged dress. She opened her eyes and flicked her hair back out of her face. Saving Father was up to her now.

Clutching Jimmy's hand, Olive headed up the street between the shops, trying to ignore the delicious smells wafting from them. She wasn't there for food; she was there for Father. She cleared her throat and raised her piping little voice.

"It was many and many year ago," she sang, her quavering little voice rising hesitantly through the air among the clamor of the street noise. "In a kingdom by the sea; that a maiden there lived whom you may know by the name of Annabel Lee…"

Jimmy hung on to Olive's hand as she sang. Song after song rolled from her lips, and yet nobody seemed to hear her. Nobody paused to listen, let alone toss a coin in her direction. Olive refused to let her voice falter, although with every person that passed, the hope that had been so strong in her heart that morning dwindled all the more.

She was halfway through the last song she could think of when, finally, someone stopped. It was an older gentleman, well-dressed, snow gathering on his hat and coat as he stood watching. He had long, white whiskers and gentle blue eyes that studied Olive with something that could have been pity. She locked her gaze on him as if she could will him to give her something just by the sheer force of her hope, and pushed her voice harder, singing with all the strength she had. It didn't feel like much, but it seemed to be enough for the old gentleman. He reached into his pocket, pulled out two shiny pennies, and held them out to Olive. Jimmy almost snatched them in his eagerness.

"Thank you!" he said, but the old gentleman was already walking away.

The kindness in the old man's eyes was as rare as it had been genuine. As the morning dragged on, hundreds of people passed by Olive's spot, their pockets jangling merrily with money – and only two or three of them cared to spare a penny for these little ragamuffins. Olive's voice grew tired, and she could hear a new rasp in it that hadn't been there this morning, but she pushed herself to sing with as much emotion and gusto as she could find within herself.

It was almost noon when she first spotted them. A ragtag gang of boys, the eldest perhaps thirteen or fourteen, the youngest no bigger than Olive herself. They were dressed as raggedly as she was, but there was something different about them, something dark and dirty in the way that they moved.

Jimmy noticed them at once. "What are they doing, Olive?" he asked.

Olive didn't interrupt her song, hitting a high note with all her might, but keeping her eyes fixed on the boys. They were slipping through the crowd almost seamlessly, like shadows among the bright colors of the wealthy. They were so quick that it took Olive a few minutes before she saw it: the flash of gold in the oldest boy's hand as he flicked a pocket-watch easily out of the coat of a nearby gentleman. Her blood ran cold.

"What are they doing?" Jimmy asked again, insistently.

"They're – they're stealing." Olive said the word in a hushed, hurried tone, as if saying it too loudly would get her hanged instead of them. "Come on, Jimmy. We've got to get out of here."

"Why?" asked Jimmy. "That man just gave us a sixpence. Maybe they'll all be friendlier in the afternoon."

Olive could see the boys coming toward them. She backed away, tugging at Jimmy's hand. "We're leaving. Come."

Jimmy pulled back. "Why? What is it?" Petulance and fear mingled in his voice as he stared up at her, his eyes huge and wide in his pinched little face. "Olive, what's wrong?"

"It's not safe." Olive yanked him closer to her. "Come!" She spun around and almost bumped directly into the oldest boy. Somehow, he had sneaked around behind her, and now he towered over, a sewer smell emanating from his dirty clothes, an angry sneer twisting his face. The first few hairs of a mustache were just starting to sprout on his upper lip, parting right and left over an ugly scar that traced a white-hot line down over his mouth and chin. Olive's heart was hammering. She wanted to speak, but her voice seemed to have left her, abandoned her the same as her courage.

"Why, ain't you a pretty little thing," the boy said, his sneer widening.

Gasping in fear, Olive pulled Jimmy back, trying to run the other way, but the boys were everywhere, closing a circle around them. There would be no escape. She hugged Jimmy close to her, staring up at the ringleader with wide eyes. "L-leave us alone," she stammered. "We just want to go home."

There was a ripple of laughter around the circle. "Just want to go home, do you?" laughed the ringleader. "Don't we all." He took a menacing step nearer. "I see you've been putting that pretty voice to work, little girl. You've got to have some takings on you."

Olive tried to shield Jimmy with her body, acutely aware of the coins in the pocket of his threadbare coat. "Nothing," she whimpered.

The boy's eyes narrowed. He planted a dirty hand on her shoulder and shoved. The force of it almost knocked Olive off her feet; she staggered, grabbing Jimmy's arm to stay upright.

"Don't lie to me," the boy spat. "Give me those coins, and I won't give you a beating."

Olive's eyes darted around the circle. There were so many boys all around her, each wearing the same expression of greed and violence. There was no way they could fight their way out of this – not one small girl and her tiny brother.

"All right," she said, tremulously, her mind working fast. She reached into Jimmy's coat – her little brother was mute with fear – and pulled out a single penny. The boys' eyes lit up as its copper glinted in the sun. Taking a deep breath, Olive held it out so that the ringleader could see it. Before he could extend a hand, she threw it to the side.

Every boy had his eyes on the penny as it arced through the air for the split second that Olive needed. She grabbed Jimmy and shoved him in front of her. "Run!" she yelled at him. "Run, Jimmy, run!"

Jimmy didn't need telling twice. He took off like a scared rabbit, and Olive was right on his heels, her breaths coming in hot little puffs as her arms swung to and fro in desperate rhythm with her pounding feet. Her toes ached with cold, but she ignored them, hammering her feet onto the pavement as hard as she could. Jimmy would never find his way home alone. She had to outpace these boys somehow. Already, she could hear them shouting, feel the pavement shake under her feet as they gave loud and furious chase.

With a burst of speed, Olive caught up with Jimmy. She grabbed his hand and pushed him into the nearest market stall. Fruits rolled everywhere as they crashed through the stall; there was an angry yell as the stallholder rushed to stop them, but Olive ducked under his arm. Jimmy dived between his legs and then they were running back down Boundary Street as fast as their legs could carry him. There were shouts and thumps behind them as the gang of boys slipped on the fruit and scrambled around the enraged stallholder, but Olive knew without looking back that some of them would still be hot on their heels. She didn't look back, she didn't look around, she just grabbed for Jimmy's hand and ran with all the strength she had.

The next two minutes were the most terrifying of Olive's life. Keeping a tight hold on Jimmy, she weaved through the crowd, jumping onto barrels to get over alley walls, crashing through some of the ramshackle homes that made up the slums, ducking under the necks or bellies of horses and narrowly missing their iron-rimmed feet as they squealed and panicked. Gradually, the sounds of pursuit behind them faded away. Olive slowed to a jog, her chest burning with effort. Jimmy was coughing uncontrollably as she glanced behind her. There was no sign of the boys.

"Are they gone?" Jimmy rasped as they fell back into a walk.

"Yes," said Olive. "I think so." She wiped at her brow, which was damp despite the chilly air. "Come on. Let's go home."

They were only five minutes' walk from home, but for Olive's exhausted feet, it felt like a hundred miles. She dragged her feet through the sludge of the streets, trying to ignore Jimmy as he complained about how tired and hungry he was. She could see her bare, blue toes through a hole in her left shoe. They grew more and more cold as they walked, getting covered in grime with every step, but it was easier to look down at them than up at the desolation all around them.

"Do you still have the money?" she asked Jimmy quietly.

Her brother laid a small hand on his coat. "Yes. All of it, except the penny that you threw at the boys." He stared up at her. "You were really brave, Olive."

Olive said nothing. Instead, looking up, she saw that they had reached their tenement building. It was a small thing, narrow and high, ramshackle, its tiny windows mostly broken. She could see the corner of one of Father's old hats sticking out of the window of their section of the building. The door hinges creaked and wobbled as they headed inside, and they had to step carefully to avoid the broken planks on the stairs as they made their way up.

Halfway up the staircase, Olive raised her voice. "Father! We're home!" The word seemed a sorry description for this pit of cold and filth.

There was no reply. Olive's heart sped up. "Father?" she called, quickening her steps. The only sound that responded was the moan of the wood underneath her feet, and Olive felt fear grip her limbs. As one, she and Jimmy burst into a run. They crashed into the tenement, and for a moment, Olive was sure her father was dead. He lay so pale and so motionless on the mattress, his rags clinging to his broken body with sweat.

"Father!" Olive screamed. She ran to him, flung herself on his chest. He stirred, and a weak hand lifted to caress her tattered and dirty hair. There were tears in Olive's eyes as she looked up, but she could still make out her father trying to smile, the muscles in his cheeks trembling with effort. "Olive," he croaked.

"Father." Olive clung to his shirt, cuddling frantically against his chest. "You scared me."

Father didn't respond. He took a long, rattling breath that seemed to be chafing against raw flesh in his throat. "Where have you been?" he whispered at length.

"Come, Jimmy." Olive grabbed his coat, pulling him closer. "Give me that." She tugged the money out of his pocket and held it out to Father with trembling hands. "I sang, Father," she said, tears spilling hot and wet down her cheeks. "I sang and I got some money and we'll get the doctor. You'll see. We'll get the doctor and soon you'll be all better."

"Oh, Olive." Father's hand brushed against her cheek; his fingertips were ice cold. His eyes burned with love and fever. "You're a good girl." His eyes closed, his breaths coming in choked gasps. "You're... a... good... girl..." he murmured.

"Father?" Olive sat up, cupping his face in her small hands.

"Father, stay awake. Come on!" She gave him a little shake. "No! Father!"

But his eyes did not open. Instead, he let out a long sigh, and his body seemed to sag, his head lolling to one side.

"No. NO!" Olive screamed at the top of her voice. "FATHER! Father!"

Yet she knew that he couldn't hear her, that he would never hear her again, that he would never open those eyes again. For a terrified, frozen moment, she stared at him, holding her breath. And yet she did not see her father, the strong man who had led her around the garden many, many months ago. All she saw was a skeleton, a shell of a shadow of a human being, a forgotten and discarded thing lying there on the mattress.

Father was gone.

"No!" Olive screamed, clutching at Father's shirt. She flung herself on his chest, tears streaming from her eyes. "NO!"

Running feet sounded on the stairs, and the door crashed open. "Olive?" The voice was Mother's and charged with terror. "Olive, what's the matter?"

"Father," was all that Olive could manage. "Father."

Mother's hands gripped her. "Get away, child." She shoved Olive away. "Peter? Peter!"

But there was no response. And there never would be again.

THE MEN THAT CAME FOR FATHER'S BODY WERE BIG AND rough. They were smoking as they walked into the tenement, and their watery eyes glanced around it with no sign of any emotion other than mild boredom.

Olive didn't want them to take him away. She sat beside the mattress, clinging to the cold, stiffening hand that had held hers so many times. Now the fingers were white and useless in her hand. The men marched toward her with a businesslike carelessness. "Out the way, little 'un," one of them grunted.

Olive's grip on Father's hand tightened. She didn't want to let him go. She didn't know how to say goodbye. "Please," she whimpered, the words coming unbidden. "Don't take him."

"Olive, come here." Mother's voice was harsh and trembling.

Olive realized she had no choice. Jumping up, she scurried over to her mother and buried her face in Mother's skirts. She heard the mattress shifting as they lifted Father's body and she tried not to look, but when they went through the door, she caught a glimpse of Father's head rolling back, his mouth falling open as they carried him off down the stairs.

No one said anything, but Jimmy and Olive sobbed quietly into Mother's skirts. Mother had a hand on each of them, unmoving, as they heard the two men coming back up the stairs. When they reached the top, Mother held out her hand to Jimmy. He mutely placed the few coins they had received that morning into her palm, and she held them out to the men.

"Thank you," she said stiffly.

They leered at her, took the money, and left. Only when the door closed behind them did Mother finally seem to break. She crumpled to the floor, her entire body trembling, and pulled the children into her lap, and the dam broke. They all clung to one another and allowed their grief to flow through them like a river of tears or blood, cascading between them, pooling in the corners of the filthy room, trickling from the cracks in the thin wooden walls, gathering and churning in the skirts of the woman who was now a widow.

"What will we do, Mother?" cried Olive between her tears. "What will we do?"

Mother dragged them both into her arms, her face white, her jaw set.

"Survive," she said.

CHAPTER 4

Two years had gone past, and all that had changed in the tenement was the level of decay. The windows gaped wider now, only a few fragments of rotting newspaper clinging to the jagged edges in a sad attempt to keep out the chill wind. The mattress was thinner, little more than a barrier between splinters and skin on the rough floor. And Jimmy, far from being endlessly busy and difficult to entertain, was a little wisp of a thing in the corner now; he hardly spoke, now playing with splinters and scraps of rags, his eyes disillusioned in his pale face as he listlessly pushed his makeshift toys around the floor.

Olive had long since stopped trying to keep the floor clean. She sat cross-legged against the wall, a dress in her lap, working on a small hole in its collar. The material was silky and soft in her fingers, a sharp contrast to the rough rags that clung to her frame. She had started to outgrow them again, but she knew that all that would mean was her ankles and wrists would be even colder when she stepped outside into the chill winter air.

The needle slipped in her cold fingers, and there was a tiny stab of pain in the bed of her thumb. Olive saw a drop of blood welling up and thrust her thumb into her mouth.

"Are you all right, Olive?" asked Jimmy from the corner.

Olive looked over at him. His face was so skeletal; his eyes unnaturally bright. "I'm all right," she said, putting down the mending. She came over to him and touched his forehead, which burned against her skin. "How do you feel?"

Jimmy shrugged, turning back to his game. "Fine."

Olive's heart squeezed with worry. She had been trying all morning to get him to nibble on the crust of stale bread that she'd been hoarding since yesterday, even though the hunger gnawing at her own stomach kept tempting her to take it for herself. "Would you like a bite to eat?"

Jimmy shrugged again. Olive got up and took the crust off its place on their single shelf where she kept it in a tin box away from the varmints. She broke off a small piece of it, trying to prevent the crumbs from trickling between her fingers.

"Here, love. Just a little. Please." She swallowed, her own voice haunting her. She had spoken to Father in exactly the same way. "For me."

Jimmy looked up at her, his eyes searching hers. She hoped he saw courage there instead of pleading desperation. Whatever he saw, he took the bread and chewed listlessly on a corner of it. "Thank you," he said.

Olive sat down on the floor beside him, putting an arm around his shoulders. "Mother will be back soon. Maybe she'll have fresh bread for us, or a piece of fish."

Jimmy studied Olive with hooded eyes. "Why is Mother gone all day lately?" he asked. "Now you have to do all the mending."

"I don't know," Olive admitted, although she knew full well that Mother wasn't getting their food with money. Everything they made on the mending went toward paying the rent. "But I'm sure she'll be back soon. Why don't you sleep a little?"

Without protest, Jimmy climbed onto the mattress, curled himself up and went to sleep. Olive stood over him, watching him breathe, a gentle rattle with every breath sounding like an ominous warning. She wished he would just be a pain again, pushing and bouncing, wanting to find a game or sing a song or do anything except just sleep. She would give anything for him to complain that he was hungry again. But now, if he wasn't coughing, he was vomiting. The grubby floor was extra stained because of this.

"I wish I knew how to help you, little brother," Olive whispered to him, reaching down to brush her fingertips across his bony shoulder. She knew she could pick up the mending and go on with it as well as she could, but somehow it didn't seem enough. Tears welled up in her eyes. She was so scared that she was going to lose Jimmy just like she'd lost Father – that she wouldn't be able to save him, either.

Footsteps on the stairs jolted Olive out of her reverie. She dashed away her tears quickly and hurried back to her corner, scooping the mending into her lap and busying herself with the needle as well as she could.

The door opened, and Mother walked in. Olive glanced up.

"Hello, Mother," she said, as brightly as she could. "How are you..."

Her voice trailed off, and fear clawed at her heart. Mother's eyes were red. Two white trails were washed on her dirty cheeks, showing where her tears had run, smeared where she'd tried to wipe them away with grubby hands. She carried the old cloth bag in one hand, but it hung loose and empty.

"Mother?" Olive's voice quivered. "What's wrong?"

Mother tried to speak, but instead, she pressed a hand over her mouth. The sound that escaped her was not so much a sob as a groan of agony made audible and ripped relentlessly out of her chest. Olive jumped to her feet, the clothes sliding off her lap, the needle clattering on the floor.

Jimmy was on his feet. "Mother?"

"I'm sorry," Mother choked out. "I'm so sorry."

She swayed for a moment, as if her knees would buckle and she would slide to the ground, but instead a new resolve seemed to wash over her. Straightening, she swallowed her tears, wiped a hand over her face and looked Olive in the eye. "Give me that, darling." She pointed at the mending lying on the floor.

"It's not done yet," Olive said softly.

"I know. It doesn't have to be." Mother sighed, bending down to scoop the clothes into her arms. "I'm not going to be doing the mending for Mrs. Clark anymore."

"What?" Cold fear shot through Olive's body. She knew that the mending money was barely enough to cover their rent every week, no matter how hard Mother tried to hide the fact from her. "What do you mean?"

A muscle jumped in Mother's cheek as she clenched her jaw. "Olive, I don't have the mending job anymore," she said. "Mrs. Clark has hired a new maid to do all the work, and she doesn't need me to do this anymore." She clutched the clothing tightly, her hands shaking, although her voice was rock steady. "I have to take this back. I will return soon."

"But what are we going to do, Mother?" Olive cried in horror. "How are we going to pay the rent?"

Mother did not respond. She was already disappearing through the door, rushing down the steps almost at a run.

"Mother!" Olive rushed to the doorway. "What are we going

to do?" she screamed down the dark and windy staircase. The only response was the sound of the front door slamming as Mother fled the tenement and disappeared onto the frigid streets.

⚜

THE FOLLOWING WEEK CAME AND WENT, AND AS THE queues formed in front of the pawnshops, Olive and her little family stood outside the tenement and stared up at it with mute longing. Olive had never thought she would ever have wanted, desperately wanted, to get back into their filthy tenement; yet now, as the snowflakes settled on her hair and hands, she would have given almost anything to go back up those creaky stairs and walk back into that drafty, dirty room.

But that would never happen. Mother had nothing left to pawn. The rent collectors had just turned them out of the only home they had, and there was nowhere to go, no other options.

Olive swallowed. "Mother," she said, in a husky croak, "can't we have our mattress?"

Mother gave her head a single, curt shake. "This is all we have," she said, glancing down at the cloth bag in Olive's hand. It contained a single, threadbare blanket. Mother's brown eyes stared back up at the tenement for a few seconds, a mixture of horror and rage crossing over her face.

"Come," she said. "We're going."

"Where are we going?" Jimmy asked as Mother dragged them off into the streets. Snow had been trampled into sludge and mixed with horse manure; it lay in off-white heaps along the pavement, pock-marked by dead rats and bits of garbage, reeking of poverty and decay. More snow was falling now, and Mother said nothing for a few moments as they walked down the cold pavement. Olive's little toe was sticking out of a hole in her shoe, and every time it touched the ground, it stuck to the pavement a little bit as it froze to the iced surface. She looked down at her toe, trying to curl it up into her shoe, but it was numb with the cold.

Jimmy sniffed and wiped his nose, coughing a little. "Mother?" he prompted, looking up into her face with open fear.

Mother sighed. "I don't know, love," she said. Her voice trembled, but her face held firm. "I just don't know."

CHAPTER 5

"Sing me something, Olive," Jimmy whispered.

Olive raised her head wearily. Every bone in her body ached with the cold and so many nights of lying on the hard, iced ground to sleep. Last night, they had lain behind a heap of rubbish, trying in vain to use the stinking garbage as a wind-break. Tonight was marginally better; they had finally found an abandoned alleyway that contained three broken barrels. Mother had dragged them into a kind of shelter, and now Olive and Jimmy lay in the nook they formed, bundled together in the stiff and filthy remnants of their blanket. The alley smelt of sewage, and where Olive lay, she could see a dead rat lying bloated on its back. Its withered little paws stuck up into the air, curled up as if it had been clutching at life at the moment of its death.

"Sing to you?" Olive whispered.

Her throat was sore, but she knew that was nothing compared to how Jimmy felt. He had been growing steadily more and more pale as the last two weeks dragged by, but tonight, his face was flushed. When Olive touched his cheek, it burned her cold fingers. She shivered, letting her hand rest there for a moment. Her heart was hammering. She looked over at Mother, who sat opposite them; Olive could just make out her face in the darkness. They locked gazes for a moment, and Olive searched her mother's eyes for something – hope, strength, anything – and found nothing there.

Jimmy nodded weakly, his eyelids fluttering as if even that tiny movement was starving him of strength. He struggled to open his eyes again.

"Sing," he whispered.

The tiny croak of his voice frightened her. She took his little hand in hers, feeling how bony it was, and gave it a gentle squeeze. The fingers twitched feebly in response, but he didn't grip her hand back. Olive tried to still the trembling in her limbs. "What should I sing?" she asked.

"Something nice," Jimmy responded weakly.

Olive looked up at Mother again. Leaning over, Mother gathered Jimmy into her arms, pulling him into her lap. His head lolled weakly; she tucked her arm underneath it, supporting him.

"Sing something, Olive," Mother said, her voice broken. "You know how Jimmy loves your voice."

Olive's throat felt choked with sorrow. What was she supposed to sing? Where was she supposed to find anything like music in this reeking alley with her dying brother? She clung to his hand in the darkness, shaking uncontrollably. Father was gone. Was Jimmy going to slip away too? Was Mother?

Was she?

"Olive." Jimmy struggled to turn his head to her. He gave a tiny, wet sound that could have been a cough if his lungs had had the strength for it. "Please sing."

She could never refuse him. So Olive closed her eyes and thought back to the summer garden, to a brighter day that felt like it was centuries and planets away now. She thought of Father tossing Jimmy up into the air, catching him again in his strong arms, and she started to clap her hands, making up the tune as she went.

She sang about the green grass and the blooming flowers, about the blue sky and the friendly sunshine. She sang about Mother's laughter, the little wooden horse that Jimmy had taken everywhere, the way Father and Mother had danced in the streets when they passed a bandstand or a traveling musician, the way she and Jimmy had run after them laughing.

She sang about the pink dress she'd loved so much that she

wore it through to the knees. She sang about the way that she and Jimmy had always managed to sneak up behind the cook to grab half an apple or a piece of orange from the table, then run off laughing to suck on it, not because they were hungry, but because it was fun. She could hear Jimmy's laughter even now, see his brown eyes dancing in merriment as Father scooped him into his lap. She sang about the two of them sitting together by the fire, Jimmy falling slowly, slowly asleep on Father's chest.

And as she sang, she let it all go, because it was all gone. All that was left now was this alleyway, and this smell, and this cold, and the terrible soft sobs of her mother, and the total absence of her brother's breathing. Because just like Father, Jimmy was now dead.

PART II

CHAPTER 6

Olive had been scared for most of the past three years, but never more frightened than now.

During their time on the streets, Olive and her mother had been robbed, beaten, chased by dogs and almost run over by carts more than once. Twice, she had watched a fever engulf her mother and believed that she would lose her just like Father and Jimmy; twice, Olive had nursed her back from the brink. Once the same fever had struck Olive herself, and she had spent a week in a burning stupor, never really awake, barely even alive. They had somehow survived it all, somehow made it to this moment where Olive had finally found her first job, yet now that she was actually standing in the factory, she wanted to run. She wanted to dash back to the broken barrels in the alleyway.

The building was enormous. Olive tried not to walk too close to the foreman as he led her through the factory, but it was tempting to huddle against him. Everywhere she looked, there were vats and machines, bubbling and clanking, a deafening cacophony of industrialization that seemed massive and inhuman in the poorly-lit space. It was stiflingly hot, the air thick and choking, tasting of some strange chemical that burned Olive's nostrils. She blinked against the gloom, trying to make out details, but all she could see was the skeletal outlines of machines and the ominous dust rising from the surfaces of the large, long tins. Everything seemed to be painted in a strange, blue-green glow. It was eerie and other-worldly, and it terrified Olive.

She wished she could reach out and take the foreman's hand; even though she was thirteen already, she felt as scared as a little child. Instead, she merely looked up at him, hoping to see some vestige of compassion in his face. Yet there was none. His face was as hard and cold as if it had been chiseled from stone.

"Here," the foreman grunted, pointing down the row of containers to Olive's left. Obediently, she started to make her way down it. Her eyes were adjusting to the gloom, and now that she was among the acrid smells, she could see the workers. Most seemed to be girls, many of them about her own age, some even younger; she could see their white faces in the dark as some of them glanced up to watch her go past. The darkness made their faces look lumpy, disfigured; they were so frightening that Olive had to look away, staring down at her feet, her heart racing. What was going on in this terrible place?

"This is where you'll be working." The foreman pointed. The long tin stood in the center of a ring of young women who gazed listlessly at Olive. It was filled with white powder that seemed to cling to everything. The sight of it and the dull-eyed workers chilled her to the bone.

"Th-thank you," she stammered, trying not to stare. She looked up at the girls surrounding the work area. They worked with bundles of wood and stood mutely, watching the foreman with nervous eyes, all but one of them. She stood with her head hanging, staring at nothing.

"You there." The foreman raised his walking stick and jabbed it in the direction of the girl looking down. "What's your problem?"

The girl looked up, and Olive's heart froze. Her face – well, she hardly had a face. Her jaw looked as though something had taken a giant, ugly chunk of flesh and bone out of it, leaving a gaping hole that wept with pus. The only intact parts of her face were her eyes: they were huge and blue, and they burned with suffering.

Olive's stomach turned as she glimpsed corroded bone protruding from the rotting flesh of her chin. She clapped a hand over her mouth, trying not to retch. The foreman showed no emotion. He just shook his head.

"Take your place," he ordered Olive. "Take one of the bundles and dip the ends into the tin. The other girls will help you. You will have two brief breaks and finish at six this evening. Do you understand?"

Olive nodded mutely.

"Good. Now—"

The foreman was interrupted by the sound of running feet. A wide-eyed girl dashed up to them, panting with effort, clutching at her skirts. There were smears of mud and dirt on her face and clothes. "I'm so sorry, sir," she cried, hurrying up to them. "I tried to cross the street and a carriage knocked me over and—"

The foreman moved casually, but so quickly that Olive heard the slap before she saw it. The girl flinched back, raising a hand to her cheekbone, which was already swelling.

"There's more where that came from," the foreman spat, gesturing with his walking stick. "Get to work. You will be fined four shillings."

Olive knew that that was half a week's wage. Tears filled the girl's eyes, but she ducked her head and said nothing. She slipped into the gap beside Olive and took a bundle of the matches. Olive's heart went out to her, but she was too afraid to speak even as the foreman walked away. She made sure to keep her eyes on her work, terrified of glancing back up at the girl with the terrible, rotting jaw.

The foreman was well out of sight when the girl that had come late gave Olive a tiny nudge. Olive looked up, surprised, and the girl smiled.

"Mabel," she whispered. "And you?"

Olive stared at her for a few moments, startled. It had been such a long time since anyone had reached out to her; normally strangers were either yelling at her or trying to steal something from her. It took her a second to find her voice.

"Olive," she whispered back.

The girl grinned. "Nice to meet you." She winked and bent back to her work, dipping the matches into the fluid. Other girls were busy stuffing the matches into matchboxes.

Somehow the brief exchange gave Olive the strength to get to work. With Mabel's arm brushing against her own, she had the strength to do it despite the smells and the heat and the awful stench of the girl with the rotting jaw. Pus trickled down the girl's chin and dripped onto the table as they worked; her movements were sluggish, her breathing loud and labored, but nobody looked up. Nobody said anything.

It must have been about ten o' clock in the morning – it was hard to tell; time seemed to be dripping as slowly and noxiously as the smell around them – when the girl stopped. She looked up, her fevered eyes afire. The other girls raised their heads to stare at her dumbly, and Olive felt a slow dread filling her soul. The bundle of matchsticks in her hands dropped onto the table with a gentle *plop*. There was a frozen moment as the girls' tortured eyes bore into Olive, blazing above her ruined jaw, imprinting their horrific image onto Olive's mind forever. Then she fell.

Mabel rushed toward her, but one of the other girls grabbed her, yanking her back. "Mabel, stop. It's no use."

"No," Mabel choked. "Oh, Jenny... no!"

"Hush," the other girl snapped. "You'll get yourself into trouble." She shoved Mabel back into her place. "There's nothing we can do for her now." She glanced down at the body of the girl, the eyes staring. "She's in a better place now."

"How do you know?" Mabel's voice was an agonized whisper.

The girl glared at her. "It's hard to imagine a worse one."

Hour after hour passed by in the heat and darkness. Olive began to feel like the day would never end, like there was nothing left in the world except for this factory. The smell of the dead girl was horrifying. It was thick and cloying, clinging to the insides of Olive's nostrils the same way that the memory of the girl's final moments stuck to the corners of her thoughts.

During their first break, when they were given some watery tea and a few rusks, Olive said nothing; neither did Mabel, but she came and sat so close beside Olive that her warmth filled the void between them, and there was a hint of comfort in it. The break lasted only a few minutes.

Then the foreman started shouting, and as one, they rose up and went back to their work. The body of the girl still lay there; some of the girls had to step over it to get to their places. One of them accidentally tripped on it, and the girl's face rolled over, and the side of her face was stained blue and purple. Olive had to swallow down a rush of nausea before she could get to work.

It seemed to be a thousand years later that their second break came. Olive and Mabel sat together, chewing on bits of brown bread. Olive's voice felt dry and labored, but the question of how the girl had died was burning in her so fervently that she knew she had to ask.

"Mabel?" she croaked.

Mabel looked up. Her eyes were red and runny from crying. "Yes?"

"What happened to ... to that girl?" She tried to ask as gently as possible.

Mabel glanced at the other girls, who all quickly looked away. Olive got the idea that there was some bad news in the room that none of them wanted to share with her. She swallowed against the fear in her stomach.

"Mabel?" she prompted.

"She..." Mabel swallowed. "She had phossy jaw."

"Phossy jaw?" The phrase rang a faint bell for Olive, but she couldn't put her finger on it. "Is that why her face looked like that?"

"Yes." Mabel wiped at a tear. "It's a horrible, horrible, horrible disease." Her voice trembled with grief and anger.

"What causes it?" Olive was almost too scared to know the answer.

Mabel turned a pair of aching, hollow eyes on her. "The stuff on the end of the matchsticks," she said. "It's made from white phosphorus. It makes you sick."

Olive's entire body felt suddenly ice cold. "You mean we can get it, too?"

Mabel nodded mutely. Olive looked down at the bread in her hand, suddenly not hungry anymore. That girl had died because of the very work Mabel and Olive were doing right now. One thing was absolutely for certain: She did not want to stay. She had to get out of the match factory, but she knew there was no way she could.

CHAPTER 7

It was summer outside, but it felt like the winter had seeped into Olive's very soul. It sucked at her bones, feeling as though ice ran in her veins, the coldness and bleakness and desperation of it all was trapped inside her every fiber, despite the warm sunshine that cascaded down on her head and shoulders as she slowly made her way home. She knew that her clothes had a dusting of the deadly stuff; it seemed stuck on her hands, too, no matter how many times she had wiped them on her ragged dress. People crossed to the other side of the street to avoid her as she made her way through one of the better neighborhoods, heading from the factory back toward Old Nichol.

She knew what awaited her at home, too – if it could even be called a home. The tenement that she and Mother had lived in back when Jimmy and Father were both still alive had been vast and spacious compared with the little place they had now. It was barely bigger than a cupboard, just large enough for them to sleep in. The building smelt of overcrowded humanity. Olive knew that their neighbors had six children in their single room. They watched her with hollow eyes every night as she climbed the stairs to get to bed.

Olive didn't look up at the crowds around her; she had made the walk from the tenement to the factory so many times that her feet seemed to know the way of their own accord. She didn't have the energy to lift her head. Her arms ached from dipping the matchsticks into that foul and poisonous tin; her feet were hot and cramping from standing for almost twelve hours on end. Yet the pain and exhaustion in her body was nothing compared to what she felt in her heart. It was as if her soul was old. Old and exhausted, and ready to give up.

Her mind wandered back to that evening. There had only been an hour left in her shift, and Olive was so tired that her fingers felt numb as she dipped match after match in that reeking stuff. She had gotten a little more used to the acrid smell, but nothing could make her accustomed to the stench from the girls with phossy jaw, from their gaping wounds. Yet even that was not enough to keep her fully awake as she worked mechanically, match after match moving through her fingers...

There was a faint clatter. Half asleep on her feet, Olive looked down to see a single white match lying on the floor between her feet. Fear jolted through her. She moved quickly, trying to cover the match with her foot, but the foreman had already seen.

"Laziness!" he had screamed, his face only an inch from her own. "Laziness and insolence! You will be fined two shillings!"

Two shillings? A crippling amount when her meager wage was just enough to buy bread and the odd hunk of cheese. Walking home, Olive couldn't ignore the gnawing hunger in her stomach, and she knew that it would have to stay there for the next two days until she was paid again. The thought was huge and aching; it made Olive's legs feel all the weaker as she continued to drag herself to a home that she knew would be empty of food.

That was when she heard it. A faint whistle; a dancing, playful thing, and she recognized it at once. It was the haunting sound of the nightingale, a sound that she had last heard in her master's beautiful garden, a long time ago when she and Jimmy and Mother and Father had walked together among the greenery and the life.

The sound of cheerful life came again, echoing around the street. Olive turned, her eyes scanning the crowd. Surely there would be no bird here; there was nothing here except cobblestones and brick walls, and a fountain in the middle of the crossing, its water slick with horse saliva.

But one person stood out from the rest of the crowd. It was a boy about her own age, and his eyes were fixed on her. There was something in them that Olive hadn't seen in a long time; something alive and dancing that reminded her of hope. He watched her, a playful smile tugging at the corner of his mouth. His lips pursed, and the whistle came again, floating across the square like a single delicious smell in the chaos and the stench.

Olive stared. Her hungry eyes took in everything he was that she wasn't: smiling, bright-eyed, and well-fed. His skin was radiant and tanned, with a rose in each cheek. The clothes he wore looked as though they had never been mended. There was a bun in his left hand, a shiny, fresh, sticky thing that made Olive's mouth water just to look at it. He seemed to notice that she was staring at it, and something that could have been pity flashed over his face.

Reaching out to the older man standing beside him, he murmured something, and the man turned. With a jolt, Olive recognized the older man. It was the kindly, white-whiskered gentleman who had first given Olive a penny for singing on the street corner years ago, with tiny Jimmy by her side—the day her father had died. The memory scorched white-hot through her soul.

The old man studied her for a moment, then listened as the boy spoke. The man smiled, and the boy looked directly across at Olive, holding up his sticky bun. Then he set it down on the edge of the fountain. His eyes were fixed on hers, dark and solemn, with an intensity that made her heart beat faster. She knew, undoubtedly, that the bun was meant for her, but something stopped her from going a step closer. It could have been fear, or it could just have been a heart-wrenching awe at the sight of someone who had so much and yet wanted to give, in such sharp contrast to their well-dressed foreman who beat the girls if they dropped a single matchstick.

The boy backed away, and Olive saw her gap. Hurrying across the busy street, she rushed to the edge of the fountain. The bun slid into her fingers. It was still warm, and its scent made Olive's mouth water as its sticky topping clung to her skin. She raised it to her lips and took a deep breath, inhaling its sweetness. Her aching stomach growled, and everything in her urged her to gobble the bun in a few bites. Instead, irresistibly, she found herself looking around for the boy. But he was nowhere in sight, as if he had come and gone as mysteriously as the angel that he had just been to her.

❦

"MOTHER!" OLIVE RAN UP THE STAIRS TO THEIR TENEMENT. They were so narrow that both her skinny shoulders bumped against the walls at intervals if she didn't run perfectly straight. "Mother, you'll never believe what happened!"

She crashed into their tiny room. Mother, who had been sitting by its single tiny window, stood up. "Good heavens, child!" she chided as Olive rushed in. "What is the matter?"

Olive paused, studying Mother for a moment. There was

something different about her today; a new light in her eye despite the deep wrinkles that the last few years of suffering had worn into her face. But Olive was too excited about what had just happened to pay much attention.

"Look," she said, revealing the sticky bun. It had taken all of her self-control not to take a single bite out of it on the way home.

Mother's eyes widened. She pushed back a sheaf of her mousy brown hair and sniffed the bun deeply.

"I haven't seen one of these in years. Cook and I used to make them all the time for the master." She reached out and brushed it with her fingertips, then looked up at Olive. There was a sudden sharpness in her expression. "Olive, where did you get this?" she asked harshly.

Olive rushed to reassure her. "No, Mother, I didn't take it. It was given to me."

"By who?" Mother raised an eyebrow. "The factory?"

"No, no. I saw someone on my way home... a boy."

Mother's eyes narrowed. "What boy?"

"I don't know. A stranger. I saw him on my way home." She paused, remembering. "He was whistling so beautifully. Anyway, when he saw me, he put this down on the fountain in the crossing. And—I knew it was for me. He looked at me, then walked away, and left it right there, and I walked up to it and just picked it up."

Mother gave her one more long, speculative look. "All right, then," she said. "What are we waiting for? Let's eat it."

Olive knew they didn't possess such a thing as a breadknife. Instead she just seized the fat, warm bun in both hands and tore it in half. Its sweet, white flesh spilled out, and she gave one half to her mother, already choking down the other in giant, ravenous bites. She wanted to go slowly and savor it, but her empty stomach wouldn't let her. In a few seconds, it was gone, only its sweet memory remaining on the back of her tongue.

But sweeter still was the memory of the boy. The boy with the big, dark eyes, and the fact that there was still kindness out there.

❦

"WHY, OLIVE," SAID MABEL TO HER ONE EVENING AS THEY rested their feet during their last break, "you look wonderfully happy today." She smiled, flinching a little. "What has you smiling so widely?"

Olive dunked her rusk in her weak tea and sucked on the end of it. "It's a strange story," she said.

"Tell me." Mabel rested her mug on her knee and smiled.

"Well, do you remember I told you about the boy with the sticky bun from a few days ago?"

"Of course," said Mabel. "He was very kind to you. Have you found out who he is?"

"No, I haven't. I haven't spoken a word to him. But for the last fortnight, he's been there at the crossing every single day, always with something to eat. Sometimes a bun, sometimes bread, sometimes even some apples – and he always leaves it on the edge of the fountain for me."

Mabel's eyes widened. "Really?"

"Really." Olive nodded.

"And you've never spoken?"

"Never."

"Why not?"

"I don't know." Olive raised a hand to her cheeks, feeling a blush creep over her face. "But I'm definitely very grateful to him."

"You should go up and speak to him," Mabel urged. "Maybe he wants to be friends."

"No, no. I'm sure not," said Olive. "Look at me." She took herself in with a sweeping gesture, indicating her dirty dress, her filthy skin, the ugly glow of phosphorus on her shoes.

"How could a well-dressed, kind and handsome boy want anything to do with me?"

"Well, he leaves you a gift every single day."

"Yes, I know, but I think that's got little to do with me." Olive smiled sadly. "He's just a good person trying to do a good thing. And I just happen to be the subject of his pity."

"Either way. I'm sure he'd like to speak to you."

"Maybe." Olive sighed. "I don't know."

Sensing that the topic was getting sensitive, Mabel changed the subject. "How is your mother?"

"She's... strange," said Olive. "She's still getting little jobs here and there, you know. Mending, or helping to man a stall for a day or two. But she's been acting very oddly."

"How do you mean?"

"Well, usually she's always at the tenement when I get back, but over the last few weeks she's been home late a few nights. She comes in too late to be working," said Olive. "Sometimes her hair is messy, too. Mother never used to let that happen. She always tells me that we're never too poor to afford neatness."

"Where do you think she goes?" asked Mabel.

"Honestly?" Olive shrugged. "I think she's seeing a man. And I don't know who he is, but I really wish she would tell me.

What if he's not a good man?" Anger flared in her chest. "Why is she replacing Father?"

"I don't think..." Mabel paused, raising a hand to her mouth. An expression of pain crossed her face.

"What's the matter?" asked Olive, suddenly nervous. "Are you all right?"

"Yes, yes." Mabel smiled, dropping her hand to her lap. "It's just a silly toothache."

"Oh." Olive felt a little relieved, but she couldn't shake a feeling of dread. "In any case, what were you saying?"

Before Mabel could reply, the foreman's harsh voice echoed through the factory. "Get up, girls!" he ordered. "Get yourselves to work."

The last few hours of the shift had always been utterly intolerable to Olive, stretching on and on as if they never could and never would end. It was during these times that the factory had always seemed the darkest; and also when, fatigued beyond comprehension, the sick girls began to faint. Some of them came back the next day, wan and pale. Many of them never came back at all. But on this day, Olive worked with renewed energy, the hours flying by as she looked forward to her walk home and her encounter with the kind boy.

She was not disappointed. Just as always, when she came around the street corner as the clock struck a quarter past six, she saw him. He was standing by the fountain, his eyes anxiously searching the crowd for her, and this time there was an entire loaf of bread in his hands.

Olive stopped on the pavement, looking over at him. He had dark hair that was just long enough to stir slightly in the cool summer breeze; his features were strong, chiseled into his face as if by a master artist. When he saw her, his dark eyes lit up as if they were filled with stars. He raised the bread and grinned, the expression as bright as a beacon.

Olive felt a sudden urge to run to him, to ask his name, to just hear the sound of his voice for once, but she felt rooted to the spot. The boy laid the bread down carefully on the edge of the fountain, turned on his heel, and walked away.

Olive rushed across the road, grabbing the bread. It was still so warm that it burned her hands a little as she held it to her chest, inhaling its sweet scent. Tonight, she and her mother would go to bed on full stomachs. Wanting to keep the bread warm, she turned and ran toward home as fast as her legs could carry her.

THE TENEMENT WAS EMPTY WHEN OLIVE GOT THERE. SHE paused in the middle of the floor, her heart racing from the run, the bread's warm weight still resting on her chest. She cuddled it closer, a little frightened. Where could Mother be?

Olive walked over to their little window. It was barely bigger than her outstretched hand, and the pane was cracked. Mother had stuffed a little piece of newspaper in to keep the drafts out. Olive peered around it, gazing down at the street outside. The buildings were jumbled and chaotic, a sharp contrast to the factory area where she worked. There, the factories were laid out in geometric lines, so neat and sharp that it made her head hurt just to look at them.

But these buildings seemed to have sprouted up like mushrooms, random and willy-nilly, surrounded by twisting little alleyways filled with refuse. Olive watched the people walking through the streets and alleys. Their eyes were downcast. Nobody wanted to look up and see the suffering of others; each one was struggling too much with the burden of their own suffering to care for anyone else.

Everyone except the boy who had given her the bread. She felt its warmth through her dress, and her heart lifted. Maybe Mabel was right. Maybe she should talk to him after all.

"Olive?"

Olive turned. Mother stood in the doorway, her cheeks strangely flushed, her eyes brighter than normal; yet there was no fever in her. This was something else. She saw Olive's appraising glance and self-consciously pulled a hand through her hair.

"When did you get home?" she asked.

"Just now," said Olive. "Mother, are you all right?"

"Of course, darling." Mother pulled herself together. "What do you have from our friend the bread boy?"

"A whole loaf." Olive held it out.

"Well, that's a mercy," said Mother.

Looking at her mother with fear and worry, Olive knew it was the only mercy they had.

She had no way of knowing that in only a few short weeks, the boy would be gone.

CHAPTER 8

Every winter that both Olive and Mother survived seemed to be a small miracle. Her hands worked automatically by now, dipping the matches into the phosphorus mixture in the same movement that she'd been doing day after day, month after month for almost two years. She didn't even look at what she was doing. She didn't look at anything. All she did was work, her eyes fixed glassily on nothing, trying her best to switch off her entire soul so that she didn't have to feel anything.

There was a soft bump on her left shoulder. She didn't have to look up to know that Mabel had just brushed against her for a moment of comfort. Olive leaned into Mabel's touch for a moment, her hands not slowing down. Right now, with Mother spending less and less time at the tenement, with the kind boy utterly gone for many months now, with Father and

Jimmy dead and buried four years already, Mabel was Olive's dear friend and a comforting presence.

The foreman's voice cracked through the air like a whip. "All right, shift's over!" he shouted. "Get off home."

Olive laid down her last bundle of matches and obediently followed the other girls away from the table. A thin murmur of conversation broke loose among them as they were finished working. One by one, they received their shillings and then headed outside into the street.

Mabel was unusually quiet as she and Olive walked side by side out of the factory. "Are you all right?" Olive asked.

"Oh, yes." Mabel looked up, smiling, but Olive detected a note of pain somewhere beneath her smile. "And you?"

"I'm fine." Olive reached for her friend's hand and squeezed it gently. "I'll see you tomorrow."

"See you."

It was always a wrench to turn away from Mabel and walk toward the cold tenement where Mother may or may not be. Especially now that the kind boy... Olive shook her head. She couldn't think about him, not now, not even though the tentative flowers of spring had bloomed into the fullness of summer. Rich, golden light streamed across the streets as Olive made her way back toward Old Nichol, illuminating first the square, the squat factories, and then the more beautiful sights of London. But Olive left the industrial district and moved through the marketplace toward the slums where she lived.

When the boy had first disappeared at the end of last summer, Olive had waited for hours at the fountain, hoping he would appear. It had taken weeks for her to realize that he had abandoned her. Then she had taken a roundabout route home, avoiding the street corner at all costs. It was too painful. She missed the boy. Missed his smile. And of course, she missed the food he brought her.

But that day, she didn't avoid that particular street corner. As much as seeing the fountain hurt her, it was easier than walking the extra distance home. The golden evening light lit up the shop windows and gleamed on the brass doorknobs as she made her way down the street. The soft music of the fountain splashed and played gently on the crossing, and Olive knew that she stuck out like a sore thumb in her tattered, green dress.

Reaching the fountain, Olive stopped for a few moments, gazing at it. Her mind flickered back to the last day that she saw the boy. He had been smiling and laughing at something his grandfather said, his face transfixed by joy. When he saw her, however, his eyes lit up even more, sparkling as they recognized her. Then a look of sorrow crossed his face. The smile fell away, and he ducked his head, reaching into a basket that he carried for what turned out to be an entire chicken pie. It was still steaming as he set it down on the fountain and rushed away, not looking at Olive. At the time, she had thought that his strange behavior had been humility about the massive gift he'd brought her. But when he failed and failed and failed to come again, she knew it was something else.

Whatever it was, it wasn't enough to make him come back. Olive shook herself, turning away from the fountain. The boy was gone, and she and Mother were alone, just as they had been when Jimmy died.

Stepping off the busy street, she moved into one of the alleyways that she used as a shortcut to get to Old Nichol. Deep in thought, she buried her hands into the pockets of her apron, feeling the greasy residue from the factory on her skin. She wondered if her dress would ever be clean again. She wondered if it would ever have reason to be clean again; would her world ever grow any bigger? Or was she doomed to move from factory to tenement, factory to tenement, steeped in gloom, allowed only a few faint moments of beauty and pain on this street corner to break the aching monotony, for the rest of her life?

She was so deep in thought that she didn't hear the footsteps behind her until they became a voice.

"Where you off to in such a hurry, hey?"

Something about the masculine voice made the hairs on the back of Olive's neck stand on end. She walked faster, knowing that to turn around would mean capture.

The footsteps sped up. "A pretty little thing like you, all by yourself in this city." There was a snicker. "Wouldn't want something untoward to happen, would we?"

Olive wanted to run. She glimpsed shadowy figures among the broken barrels in the alley alongside her, and she knew there was a gang surrounding her. She could see the busy street just ahead, and if she made a break for it now, they would catch her before she got there. Praying that the boys wanted to toy with their prey, she sped up her walk but refused to bolt.

"It's a dangerous city," purred a voice beside her. "It's not safe for a pretty young thing like you to be out alone."

Olive moved her steps a little to the right, spotting another alley branching off in that direction. If she could just persuade them that she was going down that alley, maybe she could make it to the street instead.

"Oh yes, that's it," came a third voice. "You just keep walking, little missy. Keep walking and pretending you don't know what's coming."

The sinister implication made Olive's skin crawl. She could almost feel their hungry eyes roaming across her figure, across her new curves under the dirty factory dress. But she was almost there. She could feel them closing in on her as she walked faster and faster until she reached the alleyway. She started to turn toward it, hearing their steps quicken behind her, and then at the last moment, made a dash for the street.

There was an angry yell, but Olive put down her head and

bolted as fast as her tired legs could carry her. She felt a hand claw through her dirty hair, and then she was tumbling out into the sunlight, rushing onto the street. Voices shouted and hooves clattered as carts dodged and swerved to avoid trampling her. She heard someone cursing at her to get out of the road, and she scrambled to the pavement on the other side. Looking back, she saw that she had no pursuers. She had managed to lose them in the crush of traffic.

Olive tucked her fingers into fists and ran all the way home.

"GOODNESS, CHILD! YOU LOOK LIKE DEATH WARMED UP." For once, Mother was home when Olive got there. She stood up from the corner where they slept when Olive dashed inside. Her face was filled with concern. "What happened? Are you hurt?"

Olive was too out of breath to reply. Every muscle in her body burned with effort. She bent over, resting her hands on her knees, desperately trying to breathe deeply. Mother hurried over to her and rested a hand on her back. "What happened, Olive?"

"Boys," Olive croaked out.

Mother misheard. "The boy who gives you bread?" Hope leaped in her voice. "Is he back?"

"No, Mother!" Olive straightened, her voice harsher than

she'd intended. She pushed her mother's hands away. "He's not coming back. I told you."

"I'm sorry." Mother stepped back, raising her hands. "What did you say?"

"I said there were boys." Olive swallowed, her throat tightening again at the very thought. "There were boys. They were chasing me. They – they wanted..." Olive's voice trailed off. She looked into her mother's eyes. "They were after me," she croaked.

"Olive." Mother came closer, touching Olive's hair. "Did they..."

"No. I got away," said Olive. "But I can't go back to the factory again, Mother." Tears welled up in her eyes, and she fought to keep them down. "I can't risk going near them again. What if – what if I can't get away?" She sobbed. "What if they're waiting for me?"

"Oh, Olive." Mother wrapped her arms around her. "Hush, child. Just hush."

Olive turned her face into her mother's chest and wept, because she knew she had only two options: Face the walk back to the factory and all the perils that it contained, or get fired.

And starve.

CHAPTER 9

Olive's entire body trembled with fear as she stepped out of the factory.

For two days, she had been hiding in the tenement, too scared to set foot outside. They were two days of peace and rest – until the hunger set in. There was no money for food; what little her mother had been able to scrounge had amounted to only two meals, and on Olive's pitiful wage, there had never been any possibility of saving up. The hunger pangs were familiar, but their intensity began to take Olive's breath away on the second day.

Yet it was better than going back outside. Even though she knew that she was likely losing her job, the job that was keeping her and Mother alive, she couldn't face the idea of walking back out into those streets – hearing those boys' animal voices baying at her heels. Maybe her mother could get other mending work. She was trying—Olive knew she was. But her mother didn't paint a very pretty picture of someone to hire. The years had taken their toll.

That morning, however, hunger had starved Mother of her compassion. She had grabbed Olive's arm and physically dragged her down the stairs and onto the street. "Would you have us starve?" she had been screaming. "There are worse things than what you fear!"

Not knowing what else to do, Olive had gone to the factory, where she'd been lucky to find a shortage of match girls and that she was welcomed back with a fine of only three days' wages. At least there were rusks at break time, and tasteless as they were, they filled her stomach at least.

Yet now, as she stood on the threshold of the factory and gazed out at the city in the slowly fading light, she wished she had stayed home and starved. The fear that ripped at her innards now was worse than even the agony of hunger. She could feel herself trembling uncontrollably as she balked at the entrance of the street, too scared to move. She wished Mabel would walk home with her, but her friend had been uncharacteristically quiet all day and had left for home without a word.

There was nothing else to do. She would have to start the journey, whether she liked it or not; to stay here was to invite trouble from the foreman, who would be sure to use his walking stick to give her a piece of his mind. Clutching her work-worn skirt in stained hands, Olive shuffled forward, her heart hammering deafeningly in her ears.

Every shadow and movement made her jump. Every twitch and rustle in the alleyways, every skittering rat and squeaking cartwheel sent Olive scurrying for the cover of the nearest doorway or alley. The shadows began to lengthen; the golden light began to dim, and Olive was not even halfway home yet, her progress halting and slow with terror. She had survived so much, but what those boys had in mind for her was more than even she could bear.

Her breath came in harsh, rasping puffs as she left the factories behind and started to pick her way through the marketplace and past the street crossing with the fountain. Olive wished, with all of her soul, that her father was there beside her. Or even Jimmy; he would have been eleven this year, beginning to grow up into a young man. Tears prickled at the corners of her eyes, and she tried to blink them back, but her swimming eyes seemed to be looking into another time.

And that was when she saw the boy.

He was standing by the fountain, just like he always had, wearing the same smile, the same merry intensity in his dark eyes. Olive rubbed her eyes, determined to scrub the vision away, knowing it couldn't be real. But when she looked back again, he was still there. She stood stock-still, staring. Had the hunger caused her own mind to finally betray her?

Then he whistled. The sweet song of the nightingale trickled through the air toward her. She lifted her head to savor it, loving its purity. It was the moment when she realized that he was real, and he was there. Her legs moved unbidden. She rushed forward a few steps, her eyes fixed on the boy. People yelled around her as she almost tumbled over a basket on the pavement and dashed in front of a cart in the street.

A few yards from him, she stopped as if she'd run into a brick wall. It was the closest they had ever been; close enough that she could see the dimple on his cheek, the exact disarray of his dark curls on his forehead. Never breaking his gaze into her eyes, the boy reached into his pocket and drew out something that fluttered in the breeze. A banknote. He put it down on the edge of the fountain, his dancing eyes locked on her and gave her a tiny nod. Then, he backed away, keeping a watchful eye around them.

Olive tried not to run forward, but it was hard to keep to a walk when she knew how many thieves and pickpockets were lurking on this street corner. She snatched up the banknote, gazing at it with disbelief. It was more than enough to cover the fine she had received at work.

"Thank you." She spoke without meaning to. It was the first time she had ever spoken to the boy, but when she looked up, she saw that he was gone. He hadn't even heard her.

Olive quickly folded up the banknote and tucked it into her dress. She had to get home as quickly as possible, before anyone realized what she was hiding. Her heart was suddenly pounding again as she turned toward home, but this time it was with the wonderful hope that the boy always brought with him. Despite her aching limbs, Olive broke into a run.

The streets were crowded, and Olive found herself having to turn sideways to slip in between knots of people as she headed down the street. She kept a hand on her dress pocket, feeling the thin shape of the banknote inside. There were so many people that she could hardly make out their faces. They were just a crush of humanity heading home from work, and Olive was focused on her goal.

She was across the street and almost into the alley when she felt something brush against her. Spinning around, she spotted a dark shape disappearing into the crowd. Her breath caught, and she backed away, trying to look in all directions at once. Something bumped her from behind, and she felt a hand slip into her other dress pocket almost imperceptibly. Pickpockets. Olive froze for a second, trapped by panic. Then she turned and bolted.

It wasn't long before she heard running feet behind her and knew she'd been spotted. This time there was no shouting from the boys; they were silent, intent as wolves on the trail of some hapless prey. Glancing back, Olive saw them. Four boys, all of them bigger than she was. Something gleamed like metal in the hand of the biggest one, and she knew that if they caught her, they would kill her.

She knew that to go into the alleyway would mean death. Instead she swung to the right, heading down the street. Not a single person heeded her desperate flight, their only reaction being shouts of annoyance as she pushed past them. All she knew was that she had to get away. Blood rushed in her ears, and air burned her lungs as she fled with every drop of strength she had left. She knew that it wouldn't be enough. Not with the boys so close behind, and no tricks left with which to confuse them. They were going to capture her and gut her in that alleyway.

Suddenly, a shadow darted out of a doorway on her left. Olive dodged to the side, but her tired legs fumbled, and she tripped. The pavement rushed up toward her, and a pair of strong arms seized her, yanking her briskly off the street. She tried to scream but didn't have the breath. Lashing out with all four of her limbs, she managed only a panicky whimper as she was dragged into the darkness of the doorway, the arms locked around her chest.

"No!" Olive forced the words out. "Please, no!"

"Hush. Hush!" The voice in her ear was urgent.

"Let me – let me go!" Olive gasped.

"It's me! Don't you recognize me?" the voice whispered.

All Olive knew was terror. Her fingernails raked across the door frame; she squirmed, trying to break free from the crushing arms enfolding her. Then, there was the sound of the nightingale. It bounced around the doorway, a strangely echoing music that spoke to every corner of her frightened heart. Olive stopped. Suddenly, she knew exactly who it was that was holding her.

Seeing her relax, her captor released his grip on her. She turned and looked directly into the eyes of the boy who gave her bread. They were as deep as galaxies, as bright as stars, and they took her breath away. He was standing very close.

She heard the pickpockets running past the doorway and couldn't find it in herself to be afraid. Her world had suddenly become just those two kindly eyes gazing down upon her. She wanted to bask in that attention like warm sunshine, to drink it in like daylight.

"It's you."

"Yes." The boy reached out tentatively, brushing his fingertips against her shoulder. "It's me. Are you hurt?"

"No." Olive swallowed. "Thank you for rescuing me."

"Of course." The boy's crooked smile lit up his face again.

"Who are you?" Olive whispered. She reached into her pocket and closed her fingers around the slightly crumpled banknote.

"My name is Thomas. Thomas Stanbury," said the boy. "And you?"

It took Olive a few moments to remember her own name. "Olive Wickes," she replied.

"Olive Wickes," he repeated, rolling the name around in his mouth like a sweet or a spoonful of honey. "It's a beautiful name."

Olive blushed, looking down at her feet. "Thank you."

"I was worried about you," said the boy. "When I didn't see you at your usual time for the last three days, I thought..." He looked away, his voice suddenly rough. "I thought maybe the winter had been... too much."

Olive looked up, confusion suddenly flaring in her. If Thomas had been so worried, why hadn't he helped her the way he had done last summer? "It almost was," she said.

"I'm sorry." Thomas sighed. "If only I had been here all winter, you wouldn't have suffered at all."

"Where were you?" asked Olive.

"Boarding school. I'm going to become a barrister – like my father," said Thomas.

"Is he the old man I always see you with?"

"No." Thomas sighed heavily. "That's my grandfather. My parents both died in an accident when I was a baby. Now my grandfather takes care of me, but I'm at boarding school all the time except in the summer."

"My father died, too," said Olive. She swallowed. "A few years ago."

"I'm sorry." Thomas's mouth turned down at the corners. "And your mother?"

"I still have her." Olive thought of Mother's odd behavior and of how Mother had so roughly thrown her out of the tenement that morning. "She doesn't have work, though."

"And you..." Thomas took her hand and rubbed his thumb across it, smearing the blue-green residue of the phosphorus over her skin. "You are a match girl?"

Olive felt her cheeks reddening, pulling her hand away. "Yes," she whispered, her face heating up with shame.

Sorrow filled Thomas's eyes. "I'm sorry," he said again. "I wish I could have done something for you this winter, but..." He shook his head. "Grandfather has always liked being kind to the poor, but he would never agree for us to speak. He would never take over what I do for you when I'm not here."

"What you do..." Olive's voice trailed off as she searched for words to tell Thomas what his simple kindnesses had done for her. "You give me hope," she said, her eyes filling with tears. "You are the only thing that gives me hope."

"I wish there was more," said Thomas. "I wish I could take you home. But Grandfather..." He sighed. "Grandfather barely lets me speak to the girls who live next door to us, let alone..."

He didn't finish the sentence, but the implication hung heavily in the air. Olive was suddenly and acutely aware of how dirty her clothes were, of how skinny and grubby she was in comparison to Thomas in his good clothing and flowering health. She was so far below his station that the distance between them, only a couple of feet, suddenly felt like a yawning and inescapable abyss.

There were a few moments of painful silence. Then Thomas touched her shoulder. "Let me walk you part of the way home, at least," he said.

"Thank you," whispered Olive.

THOMAS WALKED HER AS FAR AS THE BEGINNINGS OF OLD Nichol, where Olive insisted he should go back. Because he was already late to supper, Thomas reluctantly agreed. Olive was relieved. She didn't want him to see the ugly, reeking slum where she lived.

Still, as she made her way through the filthy streets, Olive couldn't help but feel lighter somehow, freer. The effect was not just due to the banknote in her pocket, which she couldn't wait to show Mother, if she were home. Something in Thomas's eyes had lit up everything that she was; she felt like every smile he gave her was a priceless gift. It fanned the tiny spark left inside her to a roaring hearth fire that bore her all the way home and all the way up the stairs of the tenement.

"Mother!" she called out, almost running up the steps, her

banknote clutched in her first. "Mother, you'll never believe what—"

She stopped dead in the center of the tenement. It was utterly empty. There was no sign of Mother, and suddenly the hearth fire that had been blazing inside her was gone. Her heart felt as cold and empty as the tenement, the thin wind blowing weak and icy through it.

Because Olive knew in her heart that Mother was not coming back.

PART III

CHAPTER 10

It had been two long weeks since Mother had left, and Olive sat huddled up on the floor where they took their breaks, listlessly sipping at her tea. For once, thanks to Thomas's banknote, Olive had gone to bed on a full stomach for days on end. Yet, there were times when she would gladly have exchanged that privilege for the warmth of her mother's body on the floor beside her, instead of the cold emptiness to welcome her home every night.

Mabel came and sat down beside her. Despite the heat, she had a scarf wrapped around her mouth; she had a toothache again, and Olive knew it was hurting her. But her eyes still sparkled with friendliness as she put a hand on Olive's arm. "Your mother?" she asked softly.

Olive shook her head. "Still no sign of her. I've been searching everywhere whenever I can, but it's no good." She sighed. "She's just disappeared."

Mabel put her arm around Olive's shoulders. "I'm sorry."

"I keep hoping that maybe she has found a job or something, some good reason for her to vanish like she did," said Olive. "But I can't help but think that maybe..." Her voice trailed off as she thought of all the ways in which Mother could be dead. Run over in the street. Gutted by pickpockets. The possibilities were as horrible as they were endless.

"Don't think that," said Mabel. "I know it's harder without her, but unless you've got proof of something bad, you have to keep hoping."

"I know." Olive tried to smile as bravely as she could. "But I'm worried about the rent. Almost all of my money used to go to the rent – Mother would find food for us sometimes. Now, I have to buy food and pay the rent." She shook her head. "I don't know how I can do it."

"What about Thomas?" asked Mabel. "Why don't you ask him for help?"

Olive felt her face coloring. She looked down at her dirty hands where they clutched her tin mug of tea. "I can't do that."

"Why not? It seems that he wants to help you," said Mabel.

"I'm sure he does, but... just look at me." Olive swallowed.

"I'm a poor match girl. He can't be seen speaking with me; it would be wrong."

"Did he say that?"

"No," Olive admitted.

"And do you ever see him at the fountain?"

"Every afternoon." Olive smiled despite herself. "He – he looks for me all the time. A few times, I've had to hide behind carts or stalls so that he doesn't see me and come up to me."

"Then what is it?"

"It's..." Olive wiped away a tear. "It's me, Mabel. Look at me. How could I go up to him, looking like this?" She shook her head. "Look at the rips in my dress. I can't even buy thread to repair it. What will he think of me?"

"You don't know until you try," said Mabel.

"I suppose you're right," said Olive. But she still knew that she would not be going up to Thomas Stanbury that evening.

❦

IT TURNED OUT THAT OLIVE'S USUAL TACTIC OF AVOIDING Thomas wasn't necessary that evening. By the time she reached the crossing where the fountain stood, he was already walking away, heading down the street to some other world where there was food and fire in abundance. Olive watched him walk for a few moments. He carried himself so straight, his feet striking the ground with a fearless definition, as if he was utterly sure of what he wanted and utterly sure that he was going to get it. His confidence was addictive, and Olive wished she could drink it in somehow. Irresistibly, she found herself following him, staying a few yards behind so that he wouldn't see her. She loved the way his black hair stirred as he walked, the squareness of his broad shoulders. Her heart ached to be in another world – a world where she and Thomas could be together.

A few minutes into the walk, Thomas stopped at a grocer's stall. Olive ducked behind a cart as he bent over a barrel of apples, inspecting them closely. Her mouth watered at the sight of them—they were so plump, so red, that she could almost taste their sweetness.

After a moment's inspection, Thomas selected an apple and held it out to the grocer. There was a brief exchange, and Thomas reached into his pocket for money. Accidentally, a fistful of coins spilled out, spinning and bouncing on the pavement. Thomas didn't seem to notice. He paid the grocer and moved briskly away.

Olive was frozen in place for a few moments, her eyes fixed on those sparkling coins. They were worth almost a week's wage to her, and she was desperate. Her desperation drew her out from behind the cart at the same moment as two grubby urchins leaped up from a street corner and rushed toward the coins.

Olive dived for them, scooping the coins up into her hands just in time; the two urchins slunk off with an annoyed look. Breathing a sigh of relief, Olive tucked the coins into her pocket and looked up. For a breathtaking moment, she looked directly into Thomas's eyes. He was standing just a few yards away, his eyes fixed on her, his crooked smile lighting up his face. Olive didn't move, just stared at him. The whole world could have disappeared and she wouldn't have noticed. Still studying her, Thomas grinned and gave her a cheeky wink that melted every bone in her body. Then he turned and walked briskly away.

Olive placed her hand on her heart, hoping she could slow its frantic beating. Every pump of blood through her body at that moment was of love for Thomas Stanbury – no matter how well she knew that such a thing could never happen. Her heart didn't know that. And the dream of it was all she had.

CHAPTER 11

Olive could barely keep her eyes open as she worked, numbly moving the matchsticks through the chemicals and into stacks, not thinking about the work, trying not to think about anything. She was swaying on her feet, lack of sleep sucking at the edges of her mind as she struggled to stay awake.

"Olive?" Mabel gave her friend a gentle nudge, whispering without slowing down her work. "Are you all right?"

"Exhausted," Olive whispered back, lifting her tired eyes to scan around quickly for the foreman. He was nowhere in sight; she and Mabel could steal a brief conversation.

"Why?" asked Mabel.

Olive sighed. "The baby cried all night long. I didn't sleep a wink – and I usually don't sleep very well between the three little girls."

"I'm sorry you had to move. Are you still living with the family next door to your old tenement?"

"I don't have a choice. I have to give all my wages to the family as it is. Four new people are already sharing my old tenement," said Olive. "Sometimes they give me a little bread. But most of the time I have to live on what we get at break time."

"Isn't there anything else you could try?" asked Mabel. "How about singing on the street like you told me you did with your brother?"

"I've tried." Olive shrugged. "I earned less than half what I do in the factory."

"Oh, Olive." Mabel looked up at her sadly. Olive noticed that her face was even paler than usual today; the scarf was still tightly bound around her face, protecting her sore tooth. "I'm so sorry."

"It's all right," said Olive. She smiled a little, thinking of the glimpses of Thomas she caught every evening as she tried to slip past him on her way home. Sometimes she succeeded, sometimes not; always he tried to give her something. "One day I will leave this factory and the tenement and all of this behind. I'll find a better life, and I'll find true love with someone – someone kind and gentle, with beautiful eyes..."

Her voice trailed off, and she clung to her dream in the darkness and stench of the factory; it seemed a fragile thing here, but it was all that she had.

"Do it, Olive," said Mabel, sorrow filling her voice. "Leave this place. Leave this life behind and go find something better."

"I'm going to," said Olive.

Mabel's eyes were suddenly locked on Olive's, burning with a terrible intensity. "Promise me," she said hoarsely, her voice too loud. "Promise me you will."

Olive was startled. "I-I promise."

The foreman had heard them. Olive heard his shoes clopping noisily up to their work station and ducked her head, hurrying back to work, but she knew it was too late. In moments, he was right beside them.

"What's this, then?" he bellowed. "Do you think you get paid for idle chit-chat?"

"No, sir," Mabel began, but it was useless to reason with the man. The foreman drew back his hand and delivered a mighty, careless slap to the side of Mabel's face. She staggered back, almost dropping her bundle of matches, and her head snapped to the side. Olive cried out wordlessly in protest. For a moment, Mabel stayed bent over, shivering in pain.

"Straighten up, girl!" thundered the foreman. "Get back to work."

Her movements tight with reluctance, Mabel straightened. The scarf, knocked loose by the slap, tumbled away from her face. Olive's entire being froze in horror as Mabel turned, and she saw her jaw. There was a gigantic hole in the side of her face, big enough for her fingers to fit inside, a terrible crater eaten away by disease, the skin ripped open, teeth and bone gleaming white among a fermenting mass of rotting tissue and oozing pus.

"No," Olive croaked. "No. Not you, too."

The foreman lifted his walking stick. Mabel's eyes, filled with love and sorrow, bored into Olive's soul.

"Run," Mabel croaked, the edges of the wound flapping and oozing as she spoke. "Run, Olive. Run."

Olive didn't wait to be told twice. She turned tail and fled, ignoring the shouts of the foreman, ignoring the glares from the other girls, her arms swinging, her feet hammering on the dirty floor. She ran and she ran. She did not look back.

THE SUN'S RAYS PLAYED OVER OLIVE'S EYELIDS, BRINGING her gently to wakefulness. She blinked slowly before opening her eyes. The warm sunlight kissing her hands and face was the only good thing about what Olive saw. She was curled up in the mouth of an old barrel that smelt like fish and beer; the ratty old sheet wrapped around her body had been fished out of the rubbish from a rich person's home, and it was torn in so many places that Olive used it more for comfort than for warmth.

The alley she was sleeping in was, at least, familiar. There was a dead cat lying a few feet from Olive's barrel, and it swarmed with ants as they covered its rotting carcass. She gazed past it and out of the mouth of the alley at the street where she had walked so many times when she still worked for the factory. It was already bustling with people; a vendor on the corner selling newspapers, a shoe-shine boy bent over a business-man's neat shoes, the hubbub of a city on its way to work. Olive could even glimpse the fountain where Thomas had so often left her bread or money. She felt so excluded from the normal bustle of life—an aimless drifter on the edges of reality.

Then she saw him. *Thomas.* He wandered into view, his hands thrust deep into his pockets, his handsome brow furrowed as he looked around. There was concern on his face; he seemed to be looking through the crowds for someone. Her? Olive crawled out of her barrel, straightening up a little. Every muscle in her body stung; her stomach had been empty for so long that it felt hollow. Perhaps she wasn't seeing him at all. She stood in the mouth of the alleyway, gazing at him as he continued to search through the crowd.

His eyes lit on her, and a smile crossed over his face. Olive gasped, realizing that he had seen her. She ducked back behind a heap of rubbish lying in the alley, shame filling her heart. Her hair was so caked in dirt that its original brown color was almost unrecognizable. She reeked of the smelly barrel she had slept in, and everything about her was ugly and unappealing. If Thomas really saw her like this, he would never want to see her again.

But she could already hear his footsteps getting closer and closer, and there was nowhere else to hide. Before she could think of something else to do, Thomas was in front of her, beaming with joy. "Olive," he said.

"Thomas." The cry of joy sprang from Olive's mouth unbidden.

"Hush." He smiled, putting a finger to her chapped lips. She trembled at his touch. "Grandfather is nearby. I've just barely managed to give him the slip – don't give me away."

"All right," Olive whispered back.

"Where have you been?" asked Thomas. "I've been searching for you for so long." Sorrow filled his beautiful, deep eyes. "You're never there at your usual time anymore. I've even gone and waited for hours at the street where Old Nichol begins, where you said your home is. But you never go past."

"I – I left the factory," Olive said quietly. "I don't work for the match factory anymore."

"Oh, Olive." Thomas's shoulders sagged with relief. "I'm so glad to hear that."

Tears welled up in Olive's eyes. She tried to keep them back, blinking them away. "What's the matter?" asked Thomas, alarmed. "Aren't you glad to be away from that place?"

"Yes," Olive whispered, "but..."

Thomas looked past her, and she saw him notice the barrel with her torn sheet inside it. Sorrow filled his face. He looked around the alleyway, horror and disgust curling his lip. "You didn't find another job?" His voice trembled.

Olive shook her head.

"So where are you staying now?" Thomas sounded like he didn't want to know the answer.

"Here," said Olive. "Well, anywhere. When I lost my job, the family I was staying with turned me out. Now..." She shrugged.

"Olive." Thomas laid a hand on her cheek, pain filling his face. "I'm so sorry. I wish I could do something for you."

Olive stared at him mutely. She didn't want to ask, but she did want, with her whole heart, for Thomas to help her somehow. After an entire month of sleeping on the street, she didn't think she could take much longer.

Thomas looked away, stepping back. When his hand fell away from her face, Olive felt something like loss.

"Here," he said thickly, his voice muffled with tears. "For you." He dug into his pockets, pulling out a fistful of coins. "This is everything I have right now. I'm sorry it can't be more." Without looking at her, he stuffed the money into her hands. "I have to go back to school," he said, his voice breaking. "I'm so sorry."

"Thank you. Thank you," Olive gasped, shoving the coins into her pockets. "But Thomas, please." She grabbed at his hands, her fear and desperation suddenly rising up to overwhelm her. "Please. Don't go."

Thomas looked into her eyes. His expression was tortured, but when he leaned over to kiss her on the forehead, his touch was inexpressibly gentle.

"I'll be back," he whispered. "I'll be back every single time, and I will search for you, no matter what."

Then he was gone, and Olive's soul rang with the hope of the promise he had given her. Yet she couldn't help but wonder if she would survive until he returned.

CHAPTER 12

Olive was on her last ha'penny.

She walked slowly through the street, the tiny coin clutched in her hand, a cold thing pressing against her cold fingers. Her eyes were fixed on nothing as she wandered from street to street, turning aimlessly this way and that, not caring where her feet were taking her. All she knew was that she couldn't stop.

It was only the beginning of winter, but already it was so cold that Olive knew if she stayed still for too long without shelter it would be a death sentence. She hadn't found anywhere suitable to spend the night, and she had been wandering since sunset. Now, the morning had come, icy and crisp, the first truly cold day of the winter, and Olive knew it wouldn't be long before the snow came. Once the snow came, that was the end of it.

She could hear church bells ringing as she wandered through a neighborhood she'd never been in before. That was nothing new; ever since Thomas had left, she had been wandering further and further from Old Nichol, desperate to avoid the place and everything it stood for. This part of London was one of the better areas she'd seen. The neat gardens in front of the clean houses with their shiny gates, the fat horses drawing their beautifully painted carriages down the wide streets – it all reminded Olive of the place where she and her family had lived all those years ago.

She closed her eyes, trying to picture them as they had been back then. Father's warm smile. Jimmy's chubby hands. Tears prickled at the corners of her eyes. She missed them all so much, and yet most of all, she missed Mother. Mother had been cruel at times, but she was a survivor; and in her own way she had fought to save her family.

She tried to think of how Mother had looked like back in those days. She had had abundant light brown hair, which she wore in a bun; her hands had been covered in sugar and flour as she helped Cook to bake and clean up the kitchen. She had smelt like lavender. Olive could almost see her now as she turned up another street. There was a church at the end of it, and the music of its bells helped her to remember a happier time. Mother had had a gentle smile, too, with sparkling brown eyes, and a smooth skin that Father always loved to touch.

n fact, she had looked very similar to one of the ladies standing on the steps of the church, about to go inside. Like Mother, this lady had a slim build, and carried herself as if she was bigger than she really was – with a kind of pride that the higher classes could seldom seem to mimic. Olive stared at the lady, remembering how Mother had always carried a hand-kerchief up her sleeve. Just like this lady. She was drawing the handkerchief out as Olive watched, demurely wiping her nose, returning it to her sleeve as she turned around—

Olive's world came to a screeching halt. It *was* Mother.

For a crystalline moment, Olive looked directly into her mother's face. There could be no doubt that it was her. Her face was not so pale and pinched anymore, her hair was longer, her frame filled out; but the mannerisms were the same, the smile identical. It was her. She was right there, standing on the steps in a beautiful dark grey church dress, her arm hooked into that of a strong man who stood beside her. She was talking and laughing with one of the other women, her face transfigured by contentment.

Olive realized that she was standing in the street with her mouth hanging open. She stepped back, anger and horror overruling the delight that had just flooded her veins. Had Mother been so happy for all of this time? Had she left Olive to get away from the burden of caring for her?

She wanted to run, to flee into the city, to scream to its busiest corner that her mother Molly Wickes was a traitor. But something deeper inside her, something primeval, stopped her. All she knew for that moment was that she wanted her mother, and she was too weak and too hungry and too tired to resist. The next thing she knew, she was running, her tired legs pounding the pavement, the ha'penny sliding out of her fingers as she rushed up to the church, her voice drawn out in one long desperate scream.

"MOTHER!"

Mother turned, her face suddenly alight with hope. When she saw Olive running toward her, an expression of joy filled her eyes, tears suddenly welling up in them. Pulling her arm away from the man, she bounded down the steps, decorum thrown to the winds, and threw her arms wide open. "Olive!" she cried. "Olive, my darling, my darling!"

Olive didn't think twice. She threw herself into her mother's arms and clung to her with all her might, sobbing, her heart hammering, her body trembling with joy. Mother wrapped her arms around Olive and held her with a tight and trembling grip that told her she would never let go again.

Their tearful embrace lasted until Olive could no longer breathe. Then she pulled back. "Where have you been?" she cried, clinging to Mother's sleeves. "Where did you go?"

"Oh, my darling, how I have been searching for you." Mother framed Olive's face in her hands, then showered her with kisses. "I never meant to leave you for so long. It was never to hurt you, my love. I had to find a better life for us. A better life for you. I *had* to."

"B-but how? What happened?" Olive sobbed.

"I left the tenement to go to the docks," said Mother. "I hoped that maybe there was someone there who knew your father and who would be willing to help us in some way." Tears filled her eyes. "Then a group of men seized me."

Olive was about to ask when the man who had been with Mother caught up to them. "Molly?" he asked, putting an arm around her waist. "Who is this?"

"Robert, my love." Mother grinned at him, her expression shining through her tears. "This is Olive."

Robert's eyes widened. "Olive?" he gasped. "Your daughter?"

"Yes." Mother half sobbed the word in joy.

"Oh, I am so glad to finally meet you." Robert reached over and clasped Olive's shoulder. "We have been searching so hard for you."

"How...?" Olive could barely croak out the word.

"As I was saying," said Mother, "when I went to the docks, a group of savage men grabbed me. They beat me half to death and Heaven only knows what else they would have done to me if Robert hadn't shown up. He drove them off, and when he recognized me as being John Wickes's wife, he decided to help me."

"John was a good friend of mine," said Robert. "As a merchant, I often saw him at the docks, and he was always a good and decent chap – not like some of the others. I always wondered what happened to him."

"Robert took me in and cared for me," said Mother. "When I recovered, we started to take walks in the garden together." She wiped away a tear, swallowing a laugh. "We've just gotten married."

Olive listened to the story, wide-eyed. How could this be true? All of this was going on when she was on the streets struggling to survive? All this had happened when she had feared her mother was dead? She blinked and shook her head, trying to wrap her mind around it all.

But if this was true, then her mother would have been dead, if this man—this Robert—hadn't have saved her. She stared at them both. Her mother's teary eyes and her ... husband's kind eyes.

"You, you saved my mother?" she stammered to Robert. "I, well, I thank you."

"I am only too glad to see you now." Robert rested a hand on her arm. His touch was gentle. "It's high time you came home with us."

Home? Go home?

Olive could scarcely conceive what that word even meant. It was almost alien to Olive now, after so many weeks on the street, after so many years of living in tiny, cold tenements. Her knees gave way under her, and she crumpled to the street, crying uncontrollably.

Her mother tried to help her up, but Olive's legs couldn't support her. She looked up at Robert.

"Oh, sir," she gasped out. "Oh, please, I will do anything. I will scrub your floors and wash your dishes and be the lowliest scullery-maid if you would just please, please help me."

"Olive!" her mother cried. "You don't underst—"

"Olive," Robert interrupted and knelt down, raising Olive's chin with his finger. "I don't think you understand."

"Don't leave me here." Olive clutched at his shirt. "Just let me be a servant in your master's house."

"Ah, Olive. You poor thing," Robert crooned softly. "You will not ever have to be a servant."

Olive stared, uncomprehending.

"We aren't servants, Olive," said Mother. "We have servants. You don't have to work. You can take lessons and get an education." She wrapped her arms around Olive. "It's over now, my darling. It's all over now. Hush. Stop your crying."

Her mother's words sank in, and the dam of Olive's emotions burst. She clung to her mother, praying this wasn't a dream. Praying it was true, and her suffering was over at last.

CHAPTER 13

It was almost a year later, on the same street with the church bells chiming their same gentle tone. Yet this time, as Olive walked down the street, she felt neither cold nor fear. The warm sunshine of summer seemed to have seeped right into her own heart, filling her with contentment as she threaded her arm into Mother's and they strode down the street along with Robert toward the church.

"I am so delighted we decided not to take the carriage today," said Olive. "It is such a pleasant walk at this time in the season."

Mother laughed. "Look at you," she said, her eyes shining as she smiled at her daughter. "You're talking like a real lady."

"I love my lessons," said Olive, grinning. "My tutor is kind, and I enjoy learning about everything. I can't believe I was so ignorant for so long. I had no idea how much I was missing – and now that I've finally started to learn, I'm determined to catch up all the time that I missed out on."

"Your tutor has told me that he's never had a pupil as avid as you." Mother put an arm around Olive, giving her a happy squeeze. "I'm so proud of you for everything that you've accomplished. You have bounced back so well from when we found you here last winter."

"I feel so much better," said Olive, smiling over at Mother. "My life has utterly changed." She paused, a small, familiar pain filling her heart. "I only wish—I only wish that I would have found you before my friend Mabel... Well, before my friend Mabel died. We could have helped her. You would have, wouldn't you?"

There were tears in her mother's eyes. "Of course, daughter. We would have helped her."

Robert leaned around her mother to look at Olive. "Yes, Olive. We would have helped her. We could have taken her in."

Olive's eyes burned for what Mabel would never experience. And then she continued speaking, "There's one other thing I really miss in this life, Mother."

Mother's smile turned sad. "Father and Jimmy?"

"Well, yes. That's not what I meant, though. I miss them, but..." Olive sighed. "I know that they've gone, and I can never have them now. No. I'm talking about something—someone—else. And maybe now, maybe with my new life..."

Mother raised an eyebrow, a knowing expression crossing her face. "I see. You're talking about Thomas. The kind boy who helped us so many times."

"Yes," Olive confessed, her throat tightening. "I am." She sighed. "I wonder how he is faring. It has been almost three years since we last spoke, yet I think of him all the time. I wonder if his time at boarding school is still going well." Her voice quietened. "I wonder if he really has come back and searched for me every summer, yet has never found me. I suppose he will have given up by now."

"You don't know that," said Mother. She looked over at Robert. "If the past few years have taught me anything, it's to never, ever give up hope."

They continued in an amicable silence. Olive was deep in thought, her mind filled with memories of the days when Thomas's kindness had kept her alive. Banknotes and sticky buns on the fountain. Even just his smile, dredging her up from the depths of hopelessness, giving her something to cling to when all else had seemed lost. She knew that Mabel, Jimmy, and Father were gone; yet Thomas might still be out there, and her whole soul and heart would always miss him.

She was gazing idly into the crowd, wondering how she could ever find him. Perhaps, though, it was better not to ever try.

Years had passed. Thomas must have given up by now – or forgotten her as a childhood folly.

The church's street was lined with trees, and there seemed to be a little songbird on every branch, announcing the beauty of summer in its cheerful little voice. Olive sighed, letting go of thoughts of Thomas, and watched the birds instead. There was a thrush giving its piping call; a cuckoo, mocking the other birds as it whirred from branch to branch. And somewhere, a nightingale was calling. Olive scanned the branches, searching for the drab little bird with the angel voice. It called again, the sound sweet and pure. It sounded as if it was closer to the ground – on a fence, perhaps. Her eyes swept the street, and they landed on the face of Thomas Stanbury.

Olive almost stumbled. If it hadn't been for the pressure of Mother's arm on hers, she would have frozen in place. Instead she kept walking, but her eyes were locked on him. He was walking through the street alone, turning this way and that, looking through the crowd as he had every time that Olive had seen him. He had grown a thin mustache and his mop of black curls was thicker; but the eyes were still exactly the same. As Olive watched, he pursed his lips, and the nightingale sound trickled out once more, the same noise that she had heard so many times on the crossing with the fountain where he had always left the bread.

"Olive?" said Robert. "Are you all right?"

"Oh – yes." Olive turned away, her heart pounding. Everything inside her wanted to run to Thomas, to tell him how much she had missed him. Yet she couldn't. Her legs wouldn't carry her. Suddenly, she was in the past. A match girl from long ago, and no amount of clean clothes and education could change that. Tears welled up in her eyes as she turned away and followed her new little family up the steps and into the church.

They found their place in their usual pew, and Olive opened her hymn book, lifting it up to hide her tearful eyes. But Mother had seen. She put an arm around Olive's shoulders. "Olive, my dear, what is the matter?"

"Nothing, Mother," Olive stammered. "It's nothing."

There was a brief pause. Then Mother spoke, gently. "That young man back there—the one you were staring at with the thick black hair. Was it Thomas?"

Olive's tears threatened to spill over. Biting back her sorrow, she nodded silently.

"Oh, my love." Mother hugged her. "Why didn't you go to him? You've been longing to see him. I don't understand."

"How could I, Mother? I'm just a match girl really. At least, that's how he knows me. I could never be good enough for him. He didn't even see me. He didn't recognize me."

"Why, of course, he didn't recognize you. But he was whistling like a nightingale," she said. "The way you told me he always did. Don't you see, Olive? He was looking for you." She took

Olive's chin, gently turning her face up. "He's been looking for you all these years. He hasn't given up. It isn't kind for you to leave him looking."

Olive was trembling where she sat. She knew that her mother's words were true. "But how, Mother? He is well-born. I'm – nothing."

"You are now an educated young lady, the daughter of a wealthy merchant," said Mother. "Any young man would be proud to have you. Yet something tells me it wouldn't matter to Thomas. He knows you as a homeless match girl. And yet he is still searching for you."

Olive looked up at Mother, her heart thundering with hope. "I-I must go to him." She gasped. "I must go to him."

Mother smiled. "Go, my love," she said. "Go!"

Then Olive was up and running, her footsteps echoing through the church, not caring about the indignant glances from people in the other pews, her fine skirts clutched in her hands. She pushed the doors open, almost bowling the usher over.

"Thomas!" she hollered from the top step. "I'm here! Thomas, come back!"

For a heartbreaking moment, she turned, looking for him, and he was nowhere to be seen. Had she missed him? Had she lost him again? No. No. No. Her heart squeezed in her chest, and her breathing came hard and fast.

"Olive?"

Olive turned to the side. Thomas stood there at the bottom of the church steps, his dark eyes wide with hope and wonder. "Is that you?" he whispered.

"Oh, Thomas." Olive rushed forward, and without thinking, she threw her arms wide. She leaped, and he caught her, spinning her around, showering her forehead with kisses, wrapping his strong arms tightly around her body. She clung to him, shaking, tears of joy pouring down her cheeks. And even though she had last known his arms when she was homeless, the feeling she had now when he held her was the closest thing to homecoming she had ever known.

EPILOGUE

"No, darling," said Olive, leaning over to help the little girl form the letter "R" on her slate. "Remember, the fat man is walking to the right of the page, not the left."

The little girl's brow furrowed in concentration. Olive let go of her hand and watched as she painstakingly etched the letter onto the slate, her small hand clenched fiercely around the chalk. That determination to learn and to do well was so familiar to Olive. She, too, had felt like that a few years ago when she had her first lessons off the street.

This little girl's face was starting to lose its pinched and starved look. She was beginning to have table manners, and she no longer tried to wear her dresses three days in a row to save on soap. But one thing hadn't changed in the three weeks since the little girl had been taken off the street: her unending hunger for knowledge.

"Look at that," murmured Thomas from his armchair. He reached over to Olive, laying a hand on hers, and stretched a little, extending his stockinged feet toward the roaring fire. His smile was warmer than the blaze in the hearth. "I don't remember ever wanting to learn that much when I was a schoolboy."

"And look at you now," said Olive, teasingly. "You're a barrister already, and a successful one at that."

Thomas inclined his head a little. "That's no surprise. I had a good upbringing. It's you, my beautiful lady wife, who should be more admired – given how your life started."

Olive nodded. "There's something about that depth of cold and fear that never quite leaves you," she whispered. She glanced again at the little girl. "She is so like I was."

Thomas squeezed her hand. "I wasn't sure about this at first, but I'm glad you took her in now. Someone has to help."

"Luckily for me, someone helped me." Olive smiled over at him. "I don't know how I would have survived those years without you."

"I'm just grateful that Grandfather finally agreed to let me court you." Thomas laughed. "I told you he'd be reluctant to let me even speak to you when you were a match girl, and he was mad enough even though you were a lady by the time I found you again. But he saw sense in the end."

"Now he can't wait to become a great-grandfather." Olive smiled, resting her hand on her swollen belly. She could feel her unborn baby stirring inside her, and it gave her hope and joy. "This little one will never know the hardship that I did," she said. "Thanks to my wonderful husband."

"Why do you say that?" Thomas shrugged. "You were already safe by the time I found you."

"In body, yes," said Olive. "But there was always something missing. I was always a match girl in my heart until you came to find me again. All those years of searching and you never forgot about me." She gazed into his eyes, her heart filled with admiration. "Only love could have done it. Only a love like yours."

Thomas's eyes, as deep and pure as the night skies, sparkled as he gazed at her. "I love you, Olive Stanbury."

"I love you, too," said Olive.

She smiled at the crackling fire, at the little girl and her slate, at her round belly that bulged with promise, at her kind and beautiful husband who had loved her when she was just a dirty little match girl. She smiled at the father who had given his life trying to provide for them, at the brother who had died in a dirty alley, at the mother who had finally found her miracle.

She smiled at the friend in the match factory who had not made it out into the light.

Olive's heart swelled with gratitude that her path had led her to this beautiful, safe moment. The words flowed from her mouth in a soft whisper.

"I love all of you," she said.

THANKS FOR READING

If you **love Victorian Romance**, **Visit Here:**

http://ticahousepublishing.subscribemenow.com

to hear about all **New Faye Godwin Romance Releases! I will let you know as soon as they become available!**

Thank you, Friends! If you enjoyed *The Factory Girl's Song!* would you kindly take a couple minutes to leave a positive review on Amazon? It only takes a moment, and positive reviews truly make a difference. Thank you so much! I appreciate it!

Much love,

Faye Godwin

MORE FAYE GODWIN VICTORIAN ROMANCES!

http://ticahousepublishing.com/victorian-romance.html

ABOUT THE AUTHOR

Faye Godwin has been fascinated with Victorian Romance since she was a teen. After reading every Victorian Romance in her public library, she decided to start writing them herself —which she's been doing ever since. Faye lives with her husband and young son in England. She loves to travel throughout her country, dreaming up new plots for her romances. She's delighted to join the Tica House Publishing family and looks forward to getting to know her readers.

contact@ticahousepublishing.com